"Fifteen years ago, I did something terrible."

"What?" Taylor asked, capturing his face in her hands, steeled for what he might admit. "What did you do?"

He read a thousand fleeting emotions in the pretty hazel eyes trained on his face. But it was the trust he saw in them that stabbed at him like a knife. She was going to despise him if he told her the truth.

He was the first to look away. "I can't tell you, Taylor."

"Sure you can," she insisted. "Believe me, no good ever comes of keeping secrets."

Her fervent tone gave him pause. Regarding her quietly, he felt as if he was looking at a total stranger. A *dangerous* total stranger. It could only be his imagination that made her words sound as though she knew from bitter experience what keeping secrets could do to a person. Which was absurd, because Taylor was the most straightforward, least secretive person he had ever met.

Wasn't she?

KELSEY ROBERTS

THE LAST LANDRY

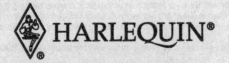

HARLEQUIN®

TORONTO • NEW YORK • LONDON
AMSTERDAM • PARIS • SYDNEY • HAMBURG
STOCKHOLM • ATHENS • TOKYO • MILAN • MADRID
PRAGUE • WARSAW • BUDAPEST • AUCKLAND

For my beautiful Katie Scarlett,
who will love seeing her name in a book!

Acknowledgments

Thanks so much to Don Scott and Marty Bass of WJZ-TV, Channel 13 in Baltimore, Maryland, for sharing their time and expertise with me!

Congratulations and many thanks to contest winner Larenda Twigg— I love the name you selected for Chandler and Val's baby! I would like to thank Pat Lieberman for helping me name Lorelei, and Helen from Sault Ste. Marie for helping name Kasey and Sarah.

ISBN 0-373-88677-2

THE LAST LANDRY

Copyright © 2006 by Rhonda Harding Pollero

www.eHarlequin.com

Printed in U.S.A.

ABOUT THE AUTHOR

Kelsey Roberts has penned more than twenty novels, won numerous awards and nominations; landed on bestseller lists, including *USA TODAY* and the Ingrams Top 50 List. She has been featured in the *New York Times* and the *Washington Post,* and makes frequent appearances on both radio and television. She is considered an expert in why women read and write crime fiction as well as an excellent authority on plotting and structuring the novel.

She resides in south Florida with her family.

Books by Kelsey Roberts

HARLEQUIN INTRIGUE

*The Rose Tattoo
†The Landry Brothers

CAST OF CHARACTERS

Shane Landry—The youngest Landry runs the Lucky 7 ranch but may have no claim to the land considering he may not be a Landry at all.

Taylor Reese—She's been housekeeper for the Landrys for five years and about to turn in her resignation...if she can bear to part ways with Shane.

Priscilla Landry—The mother of the Landry brothers has turned up dead. What secrets did she take to the grave?

Caleb Landry—The Landry patriarch was murdered. Was it a twisted romantic triangle that led to his death and that of his wife?

Will Hampton—The Lucky 7 ranch foreman is keeping many secrets behind his quiet facade.

Luke Adams—This ranch hand has a questionable past and a tendency toward violence.

Senator Brian Hollister—He has everything to lose. But is he capable of murder?

Constance Hollister—Knows all the Landry secrets and will keep them in order to protect her marriage and place in society.

Prologue

WMON-TV, News at Eleven

"Funeral services were held at the Jasper Community Church this afternoon for Caleb and Priscilla Landry, the wealthy Jasper couple whose remains were discovered last week in a dry abandoned well on the ranch owned by the family.

"Law enforcement officials have classified the gruesome discovery as an active murder investigation. Sheriff Seth Landry, seen here with his six brothers, is currently heading the investigation, though sources close to the story have indicated that the Montana State Police are planning to take over, since the victims are the parents of the Jasper sheriff.

"Detective Fitz Rollins, chief homicide detective with the state police, said in an interview following the funeral that despite the crime happening fifteen years ago, several strong leads have been developed based on items recovered in the well along with the remains.

"Among the hundreds of mourners, many prominent Montanans attended the services today, including Governor Greenblat, Senator Hollister and State Legislator Jack English. In the interest of full disclosure, we here at WMON also wish to express our condolences to the Landry family. As many of you may remember, Chandler Landry was an anchor here at this station for many years and we all send our sincerest sympathies to Chandler and his family during this difficult time.

"Switching gears now…"

"Turn it off," Callie groused as she rubbed circles on her very extended belly. Her feet were propped on a chair to ease some of the swelling in her ankles.

Taylor turned off the TV, then went into the office, returning with a pillow that she gently wedged into place beneath her friend's knees. "You look beat."

"No, I look like Shamu," Callie whined. "I'm huge. I'm gigantic, I'm—"

"Eight months pregnant with twins?" Taylor smiled as she went back to the towers of plastic containers lining the counter. "I've got enough food here to feed a developing country. What am I going to do with it all?"

"It's calving season," Callie said. "Pick out what you want and send the rest down to the bunkhouse. I think Sam said they hired on twenty new temporary hands. Those guys are always hungry."

"Good idea," Taylor agreed, opening the top drawer and removing a roll of freezer tape and a marker. She peeked under the lids in order to write neat labels on each container. "I hope they like macaroni salad."

"They're men," Callie reminded her. "They'll eat anything they don't have to cook themselves."

True enough. One thing Taylor had learned in her five years as the Landrys' housekeeper was that along with a Y chromosome came a healthy, hearty appetite.

Something that had been sorely lacking in the main house in the week since the bodies had been discovered. "How's Sam?" she asked.

The other woman shrugged. "You know my husband. His idea of dealing with anything is to soldier on. Then again, I think he's always suspected they were dead."

Who didn't? Taylor thought, though she felt it was better to keep that to herself.

"Cody is taking it the hardest," Callie added, "though Shane is running a close second."

"That's to be expected." Taylor continued labeling the containers as they talked. "Until they pulled the skeletons out of the old well and Cody had proof otherwise, I think he honestly believed he would find his parents on some remote island, sipping umbrella drinks. I think Shane just wanted them to come back. Understandable, since he's the youngest."

Callie sipped a glass of juice. "Maybe now this family can finally heal."

"I hope so. Think they're ready for more coffee?" Taylor asked, hearing the muffled voices of the Landry brothers, who were still huddled in the living room.

"Have you ever known a time when they didn't want coffee?" Callie remarked. "I miss coffee," she sighed. "I miss sleeping on my stomach and I miss being able to stand up with some semblance of dignity. Now I hoist myself out of a chair like bulky cargo being off-loaded from a tanker. I'm supposed to be glowing. See any glowing here?"

Taylor patted Callie's hand and chuckled. "Buck up. It's almost over and soon you'll have two beautiful babies to spoil."

Callie's pretty face brightened. "Kevin is so

excited." She smiled. "Sheldon the Child Wonder is a different matter. He's already announced that the babies can't come into his new room. Ever."

"He's two," Taylor remarked. "Jealousy is normal at that age. He'll be fine." She felt confident in the advice offered, thanks to the experience she'd gained courtesy of the three afternoons a week she volunteered at the Family Assistance Center of Jasper. The center that didn't have the budget to hire her even after she had her degree in hand. The university wasn't an option, either. Their hiring freeze prevented even the hope of an opening any time in the near future.

Callie was grinning. "My friend the shrink."

Taylor struggled to smile back. Barring an act of God, she'd have her Ph.D. in six weeks—an accomplishment that should have filled her with jubilation. Instead she found herself dreading the reality of what it represented. No more excuses. Time to go out into the real world. Alone. Again. She'd think about that later. For now, she was still, by default, a part of this family. Better to make the best of it while she could. "That would be 'counselor.' A shrink is an M.D."

"Between you and Molly, we'll certainly have all our mental health needs covered."

Taylor felt a stab of pain in her heart. So much for making the best of it. Molly was married to Chandler; she had a reason to stay. Taylor, on the other hand, had exactly five weeks and six days left in Landry Land.

Chapter One

"Tell me again why we're doing this?" Shane Landry grumbled a week later as some pencil-necked lab tech with a long cotton swab headed in his direction.

"There were stains on the towels found in the well with Mom and Dad," his brother Seth explained as he tipped his Stetson back off his forehead. "They were pretty degraded, but they might be useful, since initial testing revealed three distinct blood types."

Shane opened his mouth to allowed the tech to scrape the dry end of the swab around the inside of his cheek. When that was over, he swallowed, hoping to rid himself of the cotton taste in his mouth. "How will samples from all of us help?" he asked as the man packed up his shiny chrome case and scurried out of the office.

Seth leaned against his desk. "I'm hardly an

expert on the double helix. I'm guessing that if we all give DNA samples, then the lab will use our profiles to filter out Mom and Dad's blood, hopefully allowing the crime scene guys to isolate the third sample. All I know is that Detective Rollins called and asked that we all do this. Since we don't have anything to hide, I agreed." Seth's expression darkened. "We don't have anything to hide, do we?"

A quick, guilty shiver crawled down Shane's spine, but he answered, "No."

Seth seemed to relax. "Didn't think so. Anyway, it has something to do with the fact that it will take a lot of time to extract DNA from the…bones, so this is faster. The investigation is high profile and going nowhere, so Rollins is in a hurry to find something that might generate a lead."

"I'm all for that," Shane agreed. "You coming out to the ranch tonight? Taylor's making a stew. She mumbled something about it when I saw her this morning. Not that I was paying much attention to her, mind you. I've found the best way to deal with Taylor is to ignore her whenever possible." Seth smiled, prompting Shane to ask, "What?"

"Nice try."

"What?" Shane repeated, feeling defensive.

"Give it up, Shane. You're hot for the girl. And as my wife reminded me just last night, for the hundredth time I might add, you better do something before she rides off into the proverbial sunset. So no, we won't be coming to the ranch. My wife is quite insistent that you two need time alone so you'll have no choice but to acknowledge your mutual attraction. Hurry up, though, would you?"

The defensive shield evaporated, leaving a blend of fear and annoyance swirling in Shane's gut. "Hurry up and what? It isn't like she sends me anything other than the stay-away vibe."

Seth's head fell back as he laughed. "You may not be technically blind, but you are totally dumb, bro. Taylor's perfect for you. You just have to find a way past her defenses. She's smart, she's pretty, she's funny, she's—"

"Sarcastic and she picks on me."

"Part of her charm," Seth countered. "Besides, we all pick on you because you make it so easy. Back to Taylor. Aren't you curious?"

"Physically or intellectually?" Shane countered. "The physical part is a no-brainer. Any man with a pulse would crawl over hot coals to be with her. But she's a freaking genius, Seth. She's smarter than I am, she's about to earn her third degree—a doctorate, for chrissake. I have absolutely nothing to offer her," he admitted, frowning. Saying it out loud made him feel like more of an idiot. Her IQ shouldn't matter, but to a guy who'd barely made it through high school, it sure as hell did.

"She takes verbal potshots at me. *Only* me. Has since day one, because the rest of you all have fancy educations."

Seth rolled his eyes. "That's stupid. Taylor isn't an intellectual snob. Ever think she might be sniping at you and only you because you're the one she has a thing for?"

"No," Shane admitted candidly. "In five years she hasn't dropped a single hint in that direction. You're way off base, bro."

"Have you?"

Over the messy pile of files, Shane fired a hostile glance in his brother's direction. "We're getting a little personal here."

"You're getting a little avoidance here," Seth retorted, his tone and cadence mimicking Shane's. "I'm just suggesting that you act while you still have a chance. Just exactly how long do you think Taylor will hang around after graduation?"

Shane didn't want to think about that. She had become such an integral part of his life.

Every one of his days for the last five years had begun and ended with Taylor. She was as much a part of the ranch as he was. He didn't want to imagine waking up to anything other than the smell of fresh coffee wafting up to his room. Or the thrill he felt when he walked downstairs to find her working in the kitchen or sitting at the table, her pretty face buried in a book.

He slumped in the chair. Shane knew to the second just how much time he had left. In 960 hours Taylor would get her degree.

"How long?" Seth pressed.

"Doesn't look too good. She never says anything, but I know she's been sending résumés all over the country. As far away as California." Shane rubbed the stubble on his chin. "The last few weeks, with the news, the funeral and the state police crawling all over the ranch, she hasn't said much. She's got to be getting offers, though. Hell, for all I know she's already accepted a job in Outer Mongolia."

"Then give her a reason not to leave," Seth suggested.

"Like what?" Shane snapped, annoyed by the feeling of utter helplessness that settled over him whenever he thought about her impending departure. "'You know that doctorate you've spent the last five years earning? Well, instead of working in your field, want to stick around, clean my house and cook for me?' Right, that'll work."

"No, jerk-face," Seth breathed. "Give her a personal reason. Like telling her that you're in love with her."

Shane stilled. "No way."

One of Seth's dark brows arched in challenge. "Because it isn't true?"

"No, because I'm not hanging myself out there when I have no idea how she feels. Hell, try *if* she feels."

Letting out a loud breath, Seth shook his head a few times. "What's the worst thing that can happen if you go for it?"

A humorless sound gurgled in Shane's throat. "She can verbally shred me to pieces, then laugh in my face. Pass, thanks. Besides, now isn't the best time to—"

"There is no best time," Seth interrupted, mildly irritated. "Look at Savannah and me. We got together under pretty impossible circumstances."

That much was true.

"You shouldn't use finding Mom and Dad's remains as an excuse to keep living your life in neutral," Seth added.

"I'm not." *Much,* Shane amended silently.

Then again, he was haunted by a demon that none of his brothers even knew existed.

"C'mon, Shane. Are you trying to tell me that you didn't suspect their being dead was a possibility all these years? We may not have talked about it openly, but I think deep down we all knew it was the most logical explanation for their disappearance."

"I know. You're right," he sighed. "I just hope the state police can find the scumbag who killed them."

"Me, too," Seth agreed, his dark eyes sparked with anger. "It's making me nuts to be cut out of the loop. Detective Rollins isn't sharing squat about his progress. I do know he subpoenaed old bank records. Makes sense. It's what I'd do, since we've always known about the hundred grand withdrawn the day they went mis…er, died."

"I've always heard you're supposed to follow the money."

"Pretty much. Perhaps you've also heard the expression 'the heart wants what it wants when it wants it'?" Seth said, back to the other subject like a fricking bulldog with a bone.

"Um, only from girls."

He might have his hands tied about helping to solve the case of their murdered parents, but big brother Seth was doggedly hot on the trail of his baby brother's nonexistent love life. "Brat. I'm serious. Look, Shane. You've got a choice to make. You can do nothing and live a lifetime of regret. Or you can decide she's worth it and take a chance."

"Easy for you to say. You're not the one facing verbal castration." Shane blew out a breath and made a production of tightening the leather strap keeping his hair in place. Grudgingly, he knew Seth's strategy had some merit. Taylor was smart and funny. But she wasn't just pretty, she was beautiful. Stop-in-your-tracks, heartbeat-skipping stunning. She was tiny, but not the anorexic kind of scrawny. No, Taylor had curves. Soft, supple curves that even those bulky sweaters she was so fond of wearing couldn't conceal.

She was perpetual energy, with sparkling hazel eyes and hair the color of winter wheat. She was also mere weeks from completing her graduate work.

"You're frowning," Seth remarked.

"She scares me," he admitted. "Taylor and I have lived under the same roof for five years and we've fallen into this…this…I don't know what you'd call it."

"The Country Girl."

"Excuse me?" Shane asked, meeting his brother's dark eyes.

"It's a movie. Grace Kelly was in it?"

"*You're* a country girl," Shane teased. "Jeez, we marry you off and now you're quoting chick flick titles. That's just wrong, Seth. You need to go out and do something manly before it's too late."

"I'm making a point, bozo. Listen and learn. In the movie, the husband is a schmuck, the wife is an actress and the director has the hots for the actress-wife. The drunk, schmuck husband gets that the director is lusting after his wife."

"What a loser."

"Whatever," Seth grumbled. "At one point in the movie, the drunk husband says the only thing worse than two people making eyes at each other is two people trying *not* to."

"And your point is?"

"You and Taylor are the actress and the director. I see the way you watch her when you think she isn't looking."

"Everybody watches her. That doesn't mean anything."

"So what are you afraid of?" Seth asked pointedly.

"Aside from the fact that she's smarter than

I am? More educated? Hasn't so much as hinted that she's interested, you mean?"

Seth nodded. "Besides all that."

"I don't have anything to offer her. What's she going to do on the ranch, show inkblots to cattle all day?"

Seth snorted. "First, you are a smart guy. Secondly, who cares what degrees she has? Thirdly, you haven't so much as asked her out on a date. Maybe you should start there."

"A date?" Shane repeated, as if the word was new to him.

"Dinner, a movie? Surely you remember how to date."

"I know how to date. You're the one who's turned into girlie, movie-quoting guy."

"I don't know if I'd cast aspersions, Shane. Not when you're celibate guy."

Shane uttered a mild curse as he left the office. Problem was, he wasn't completely sure which one of them he was consigning to the fires of hell.

"LANDRY RESIDENCE."

"Taylor Reese?"

"Speaking." Taylor couldn't tell if the voice on the other end of the phone was male or female. No response. Which was darn annoying since she was elbow deep in pastry dough. "*Hello?* Who is this?"

"Doesn't matter."

She rolled her eyes as she trapped the cordless phone between her head and shoulder in order to continue rolling out the pie shells. She didn't have time for some teenager making prank calls on a rainy spring afternoon. "It does to me," she said. "I'm in the middle of something. FYI, pal, this is the sheriff's house. If you're so much as thinking about harassing me, forget it. But have a nice day."

"I know who you are."

Was that supposed to be scary? "I got that when you used my name." *Annoying little creep.* While she could sympathize with some poor kid stranded in what to a teenager would be the mind-numbing solitude of Jasper, Montana, she had pies to bake and deliver to the bunkhouse before leaving to make her seven o'clock class. "Bye-bye."

With flour-dusted fingers, she grabbed the phone, pressed the off button and went back to work.

Not an easy chore, since the counters at the Lucky 7 Ranch were just a bit too high. She had to get on tiptoe in order to roll out the top crust.

The century-old kitchen was a cook's delight.

In fact, everything about the house appealed to her. Everything up to and including its occupant.

Shane Landry appealed to her in a lot of ways. Too many. Which was why she did her level best to keep her distance. She'd worked too long and too hard to do otherwise. She was *not* going to turn into a woman like her mother. Not going to repeat the pattern she'd learned at the feet of a master. She attacked the dough with gusto as she mentally reviewed her mother's choices. Taylor had made that promise to herself on her thirteenth birthday. Until she had created a life for herself, no man was welcome as anything more than a temporary diversion. *She'd* never be dependent.

Which was why Shane was such a dangerous temptation. *Temptation* being the operative word. It seemed unfair that one man should be given so many gifts. She frowned at her own lack of self-restraint. No good would or could come of fantasizing about him.

Though she was weeks from graduation, she hardly needed an advanced degree to diagnose the fact that she was attracted to the wrong man. She blew out a breath of frustration as she lifted the crust on top of the sliced apples and began crimping the edges with a vengeance.

"Killing it or cooking it?" Shane asked when he sauntered into the room a second later.

His large hand snaked around her, snatching a slice of apple out of the pie before she could stop him. She slapped his fingers. The quick, fraction-of-a-second contact was all it took for her pulse to kick into gear. *Damn! No touching,* she reminded herself. Thinking about him was bad enough. Physical contact with Shane made her almost forget why he was off-limits.

She nudged him back with her elbow. Did the blasted man always have to stand so close? "Stick your hands in my food again and I'll kill you *and* cook you. Not necessarily in that order. Don't you have someplace to be? Other than here?" *Where I won't smell the fresh scent of soap mingling with your cologne? Where I won't feel the warmth of your body or know that all I have to do is turn around to be in your arms?*

"I belong here," Shane reminded her. Taylor frowned again when she noticed a new bruise on his wrist as he stole another apple slice and his arm brushed hers. "You're in a particularly nasty mood today," he said cheerfully. "What happened, did they cancel *Dr. Phil?* Bummer."

"Do not mock Dr. Phil," Taylor insisted, stepping away before she turned to glare up at him. "He's a very insightful, intelligent man. Two things, by the way, you are not."

"But I'm the man who pays you, so how about something to eat?"

"Sure. Put on your shoes and socks and go to the fridge."

His crystal-blue eyes glinted with humor. "Housekeeper, Taylor. From the ancient Greek phrase meaning 'keep the people in the house happy.' This is me…" he paused and waved his hands "…not happy."

"And this is me…" she gave him her brightest smile "…not caring."

He couldn't help but watch as she put the pie in the oven, stiffened her spine and walked out of the room with all the airs and dignity of royalty departing the throne. There was the added bonus of seeing her hips sway with each step. Taylor had a killer body. She kept him awake nights. Which sucked, since there wasn't a damn thing he could do about his attraction to her. Seth's sage advice aside, Shane still didn't think he was ready to hang himself out there just to have her slice him to shreds with that sharp tongue and even sharper mind. Especially not when she'd practically just called him stupid.

Shane took a few minutes to clean up her baking mess, then rummaged around, finally settling on some cheese and crackers. There was a wonderful smell coming from the Crock-Pot, so he knew better than to spoil his appetite. In addition to her physical perfection, Taylor was a really great cook. He tried to tell himself that he'd kept her on for that reason and that reason alone after Sam, Callie and the kids had moved out last fall.

After that, there really wasn't a need for live-in help. Not when it was just him. And Taylor.

And enough sexual tension knotting his gut to choke several of his prize bulls.

He took the same seat at the kitchen table that had been his since he'd graduated from a high chair. He cut off a hunk of cheese and slipped it into his mouth, chasing it with a long swallow of beer.

He was still sad over the recent confirmation that his parents were gone. It didn't make sense. Who would have wanted to kill them?

He took a healthy slug of his beer, enjoying the whiff of pot roast and the mouthwatering aroma of hot apple pie.

Shane had a feeling his mom would have adored Taylor. And—God—she would have loved all her grandbabies, too. It was sad to realize his parents would never be a part of their grandchildren's lives. It wasn't fair, he thought grimly.

Shane focused on being happy for all his brothers. He adored his sisters-in-law and all the little Landrys they had produced. He felt like the odd man out, though. Again.

As the youngest of the seven sons of Caleb and Priscilla, he also held the dubious distinction of being the only one who had rebelled as a teenager. The only one who had inspired the ire of their father and the protection of their mother.

Shane suffered a familiar pinch in his chest. Suddenly, the snack wasn't all that appetizing, so he shoved it nearer the center of the large oak table that dominated the room, and concentrated on his beer.

Thinking about the recent loss filled him with guilt. He knew something about the time just before their murder. Something he'd never been able to share. Not with his brothers, not with anyone. It was gnawing at his insides.

Chapter Two

Taylor liked the structure of her life. A life, she acknowledged, as she carried the heavy tray stacked with pies toward the bunkhouse, that didn't fit any of the criteria she'd so carefully defined. "How did I manage to mess up so royally?" she whispered as she trudged across the moist ground, doing her best to balance the tray and avoid a huge mud puddle courtesy of the early snowmelt.

Didn't matter. It would be history soon. She'd get back on track. She'd forget that she actually liked caring for a family—lessons learned and reinforced over and over during her tenure on the ranch. She couldn't erase the last five years. Probably wouldn't even if she could. It would mean forgetting how much she loved preparing meals, planning parties and celebrating milestones, and she didn't want to do that. But she couldn't make that her whole life, right? No. Career had to be the focus. That was the smart choice. Relationships couldn't be controlled, and had the ability to evaporate in a second. She didn't want to be one of those sad women sitting alone in some dingy apartment, pining for a man. Men made you desperate and she'd had enough of desperate to last a lifetime.

So, while she liked her current life, Taylor knew it had to end. Time to move on. Captain her own ship. Float her own boat. "When did I become the queen of the nautical metaphor?" she grumbled, sidestepping another hazardous mud puddle.

Here she was, on the brink of checking off one of the major things on her life-goals list, and she wasn't happy. That was annoying as sin. She should be ecstatic, exuberantly anticipating her future.

A future that didn't include the large, loving Landry family. Taylor felt a chill carried on the early evening air. Within a week of meeting the Landrys, all of her preconceived notions had started to crumble. Everything, *absolutely everything,* she'd been living, breathing, believing, planning and plotting for much of her life had collapsed, crumpled, shattered. It wasn't supposed to be like th—

She screamed, nearly pitching the tray,

startled by seeing two men lurking in the shadows. Her yelp of alarm brought four or five more men out of the bunkhouse, along with the attention of the shrouded figures. Her heart was racing even after she recognized one of the men.

Nervous laughter spilled from her as Will Hampton stepped into the beam of light caused by the flood lamp mounted above the front door. "You nearly scared me to death!" she chided.

"Sorry, ma'am," he replied with a tip of his tattered hat.

Will was a walking cliché, the very image of a taciturn cowboy. From the hat to his craggy, leathery face, jeans, bowed legs and scuffed boots—you name it, he had it. Along with a personality that bordered on nonexistent. He barely ever spoke, and when he did, it was in one- or two-word sentences that almost always ended in a polite "ma'am."

Smiling, Taylor acknowledged the other man. He wasn't familiar, but they were at the launch of the spring calving season, so there were any number of men drifting in and out of steady employment. "I brought you dessert." She handed the tray to Will, glad to rid herself of its weight, and smiled at the other man. "Hi, I'm Taylor."

"Luke Adams," he stated, offering her a perfect smile.

Too perfect, she thought. Ranch hands didn't normally spend that kind of money on cosmetic dentistry. Nor, she noted, did they have tattoos across their knuckles. Nor, ink marks aside, were they usually so attractive. Luke didn't have the sun-aged skin of a tenured hand. He was just shy of six feet, with neatly trimmed hair—what she could see of it beneath his hat—and light eyes. Maybe he was just what she needed to get her mind off Shane. Not the brightest approach to filling her final weeks on the ranch, but it wasn't as if she had any plans for a future here.

"Welcome to the Lucky 7."

"Thank you," he said politely.

"When did you sign on?"

"A couple of days back," Luke answered.

He had a nice voice—not as deep as Shane's—and he was definitely checking her out. "Where'd you work before?" Taylor's curiosity was, pathetically, only marginally piqued.

"Here and there," he said with a shrug of acceptably muscled shoulders. Shane's were broad and sculpted. She knew this because she'd seen him shirtless. A half-dressed Shane was a thing of beauty.

"…Mrs. Landry?"

She shook off her Shane-brain and asked Luke to repeat the question.

"Are you Mrs. Landry?"

"I'm not," she answered quickly, hating that she hated saying it. "But there are six of them around. Can't help but run into one eventually."

"Six wives? Is this one of those pluralist families I've read about?"

"We gotta go, Luke," Will interrupted, clearly irritated by the mildly flirtatious tone of the conversation. "Ma'am."

Then again, everything about Taylor seemed to irritate Will. They hadn't exactly bonded during her time at the ranch. At first she'd tried killing him with kindness, but that didn't get her too far. Now she just settled for civil exchanges whenever the two of them shared the same space.

Taylor couldn't fathom why it was that Shane adored Will. As she walked back to the house, she recalled the countless times he had praised the foreman, who'd been working at the ranch in some capacity or another for more than forty years. She suspected Shane thought of the older man as a substitute father. Made perfect sense, considering that Will had stepped in to handle things during Shane's father's absence. Good thing, too, since none of the other brothers had any interest in the actual day-to-day running of the ranch.

She thought about the gaggle of Landry men. Sam preferred the world of high finance. Seth and Cody were in law enforcement, Seth as the sheriff of Jasper and Cody as a federal marshal. Chance was a doctor, a general practitioner in town. Clayton had a law office in Missoula, crusading to save others from the horrible ordeal that had robbed him of four years of his life. And Chandler, well, he was a big, important author now. Taylor smiled, remembering how stunned she'd been to learn of his well-hidden, secret persona.

Shane was the homebody. He adored everything about the ranch, including Will, who he obviously looked to as a friend and mentor. That alone was almost enough of a reason for Taylor to keep trying with the crusty old guy. She had a pretty good idea of what it must have been like for Shane to return to the Lucky 7 after so many years, only to find his parents gone.

Now he knew they were dead. She felt great empathy for the Landry clan. Especially Shane, since she knew precisely how he was feeling even if they never talked about that sort of thing. Actually, they never talked, period.

The concept of parental abandonment hit

close to home, Taylor acknowledged as she stepped off the pathway in order to avoid another mud puddle. She knew what it felt like from firsthand experience.

That was only a minor reason why Shane was off-limits. In addition to a strong physical pull, she suspected, they had too much else in common. They had—

Taylor didn't get to finish her thought. Not when she found herself suddenly flying face-first into a deep puddle of mud. Turning her head to the side just in time, she spat out grit, then let loose a colorful curse.

She opened one eye to see a pair of size thirteen boots inches away from her nose. "Is that any way for a lady to talk?" Shane chided.

"Are you going to help me?" she demanded, glaring up at him as she struggled to her hands and knees in the cold slime.

His face contorted in what she was sure was a very gallant attempt to keep from laughing. "Only if you ask nicely."

She glared daggers up at him, feeling the globs of mud slide down the front of her shirt and into her bra. "I would rather gnaw off my own muddy tongue."

"Suit yourself," he sighed, shifting his weight and crossing his arms over his chest.

Taylor did a humiliating *Three Stooges* thing where she'd almost make it, then lose her footing and fall again. But she refused to ask for his assistance. Arrogant and…stupid. Neither of those things normally described her, yet Shane seemed to bring them all out in spades.

With the grace and balance of a two-legged giraffe, she finally pulled herself out of the puddle and back onto dry land. She was soaked, and filthy, smelled like earth and was so cold her teeth started to chatter.

Shane mumbled something unflattering about her being hardheaded as he removed his coat and placed it around her shoulders.

"It'll get ruined," she complained.

"So will you, if you don't get out of those wet things before you catch cold."

She wrapped herself in the coat, feeling the warmth of his body transfer to hers. "You don't catch a cold from the weather. A cold is a virus and—"

"Can't you *ever* just say thank-you?" he grumbled as he took her by the elbow and led her toward the back door.

She practically had to jog to keep pace with him. Shane didn't seem to realize that their height difference meant she had to take two steps to his one. "Sure. Thank you for not helping me out of the puddle."

He chuckled softly. As always, the sound comforted her in ways it shouldn't and at a time it shouldn't.

"You're a real smart-ass, Taylor."

"One of us has to be smart," she retorted, glancing up to bat her eyelashes at him. "Get the door so that I don't have to wash the mud off it in the morning."

"A competent housekeeper wouldn't wait until morning." He reached around her and grabbed the knob, then yanked open the door.

"A competent housekeeper wouldn't work for the pittance you pay me." Which was totally unfair, she acknowledged rather guiltily. Sometimes she had to find ammunition when no ammunition was available.

"Free room," he reminded her, following her inside. "And board, tuition payments and a car. I don't see where you're so bad off."

Removing the coat, she held it out to him as if she was handing him a giant cootie. "*I* am perfect. *You* are bad off."

"Really?" Using his coat like protective gloves, he grabbed her by the shoulders, spun her around and marched her into the hallway.

Taylor almost shrieked when she caught

sight of her reflection in the beveled mirror above the highboy. Her hair was nothing but limp, brown clumps. The only part of her face not covered in mud were her eyes, making her look like some nocturnal creature.

"Not so perfect now, eh?"

"You're an evil man," she cried, twisting free and racing off to her room. She'd worry about the mud tracks on the polished wood floors after she showered and threw her clothes in the trash. Only now there was very little hope of making her class on time. That great, structured life of hers had gone to hell in a handcart rather quickly.

Ten minutes later, a freshly showered Taylor was racing around, putting on her shoes while making an attempt at maneuvering the hair dryer one-handed. It wasn't the best system, so she gave up, grabbing a large clip off the vanity and twisting her clean but soaking hair into a messy bundle at the back of her head.

At least she wouldn't be stuck in a class for three hours wearing a damp sweater, smelling like wet wool. Glancing over at the clock, she grabbed her keys and dashed toward the front door. If she ignored the posted speed limit and parked illegally, she'd only be ten or fifteen minutes late.

"I'm leaving!" she called out, skating on her towel to clean the mud off the floor as she went.

"For good, I hope?" Shane asked as he came out of the living room and leaned against the jamb.

She smiled. "Soon enough, but for now, you'd be lost without me, Shane."

His eyes met hers. "Very true."

Man, she hated it when he did that! Banter worked. Moments of genuine kindness, like sacrificing his coat and cleaning the kitchen after her pie baking marathon, did not. The man didn't play fair.

It was easier to spar with Shane than to acknowledge his good side. Well, technically, it was a great side. But she was in too much of a hurry to deal with all that right now. "N-night," she stammered awkwardly, moving in a wide arc to avoid even the possibility of making physical contact.

"Do you have pencils and paper?" he asked, moving into her path.

"It's graduate school, Shane, not kindergarten."

His dark head tilted to one side; his warm, minty breath fell across her upturned face. Taylor's pulse quickened as his fingers reached out, hovering just shy of her throat. Anticipation rushed through her system. Contradictory thoughts—*Please touch me! No, don't touch me!*—ping-ponged in her mind. She struggled to keep from betraying herself completely.

Not an easy task when she was standing in the shadow of more than six feet of absolute male perfection. His soft, cotton shirt hugged every inch of corded muscle, outlining his broad shoulders and solid torso. She tried not to notice that unlike her, his chest rose and fell rhythmically, evenly. She had to stand her ground. She knew Shane well. Suspected he would pounce at even the smallest slip in her facade.

That was her fault. She was the one who'd put that tightrope between them. The cute-banter idea had seemed safe when she'd first arrived at the ranch and felt the tingle when he'd shaken her hand. Now it was a flimsy cover barely protecting her from the intensity of his gaze. The longing churning in her belly. The need building day by day, hour by hour, second by second.

He tucked a strand of her hair behind her ear, making her shiver. "You could stay here. I'll draw some inkblots and you can analyze me."

She slapped his hand away. "Pass, thanks. I

don't have time to play games with boys in men's clothing." She checked her watch, using that as an excuse to divert her eyes from the tractor beam of his gaze.

"Chicken?" His tone was low and far too sexy for her comfort level.

"No, thanks, I've eaten." She inched past him. "Good night, Shane."

"Have a good time." His voice was now laced with something that managed to be seductive and taunting all at the same, confusing time. She was glad to be making an escape and even happier to have an excuse to do it quickly.

The man was annoying. He was impossible. "He does have a great butt," she murmured as she opened her car door. That small confession brought a smile to her lips.

A smile that vanished the instant she saw the threatening note attached to her seat by the glistening blade of a knife.

Chapter Three

Knife in one hand, Taylor read the note. Dread settled in the pit of her stomach. The block printing made it impossible for her to identify the writer, but the contents and the knife made the message frighteningly clear: "SHANE DID IT. THE PROOF IS IN THE ATTIC."

OhGodohGodohGod! This wasn't possible. Shane was a lot of things, but not a killer. Sure, they had their tense moments, but she knew with absolute certainty that he was incapable of hurting anyone. Especially not the mother he worshiped and the father he revered.

Why accuse him?

Oh, God. Who could have delivered this?

Maybe it was a joke. A sick, perverted and cruel one, but some fool's idea of humor. She couldn't show Shane. Not now.

Observing him these last few weeks, she

knew where he was on the bereavement scale. The initial denial stage had passed the second he'd identified his mother's wedding ring. The anger stage had passed as well, probably because he'd transferred those emotions to the fantasies of what he'd do when the killer was caught. The funeral ritual had been an outlet for the bargaining and depression stages.

Shane had now reached the final phase—acceptance. Yes, she knew it had been a sudden, unwelcome and painful journey, but she wasn't about to let some weasel with a warped sense of humor set him back to square one. Crumpling the note, she decided when and if she ever found the prankster, she'd kick him, then charge him for repairing the puncture left by the knife. "Jackass," she muttered.

Taylor heard the sound of an approaching car and hurriedly put the knife and crumpled note inside her purse. Tossing her bag on the passenger seat, she slipped behind the wheel.

Seth's marked SUV pulled alongside her sedan just as Taylor turned the key, starting the engine. With a wave of her hand, she rushed off before he noticed anything was amiss. Amiss? She almost choked. That wasn't the word for it. Amiss didn't come close to describing the protective surge of anger churning her insides.

SHANE WAS IN THE PROCESS of grabbing another beer when he heard the front door open and close. For a split second, he let himself hope that it might be Taylor coming back inside. Maybe she'd decided to abandon her class in favor of spending the evening with him. Yeah, sure. *That* was about as likely as fish learning to dance. Acknowledging that reality made him scowl.

Seth strolled into the kitchen. "Hey," he said by way of greeting. "What's with Taylor?"

Shane shrugged. "Don't know. I never know, which probably explains why we've lived under the same roof for five years and I still don't know her middle name."

"Sophia," Seth replied with a brotherly sneer as he weaved toward the kitchen. "Put us all out of our misery and make your move. Get proactive, will you?"

"Proactive? Is that from your word-of-the-day calendar? You weren't here a few minutes ago. If you were, you'd rethink your belief that she's hot for me. She thinks I'm a moron."

"You can be a moron, but that's beside the point," Seth teased. "Trust me on this, Shane. Time's a-wastin'."

"Why do you think she's interested in me?"

"My exceptional talents for deduction."

"Really?" Shane asked, smacking Seth's Stetson off his head. "Maybe you should put those skills of yours to good use by trying to figure out why the woman can barely keep a civil tone in my presence. She hates me."

"You're so wrong," Seth stated, tossing his hat onto the table. "Men are such jerks."

"First you quote movies, now this?" Shane demanded. "You are such a girl."

"No, I'm insightful," his brother said easily. "One of the many advantages of age and experience, bro."

"Do you have a valid reason for being here?" Shane asked as he watched his brother help himself to a bottle of water, tucking it into the utility belt clipped at his waist. "By *valid* I mean something more than a roadie of water and an opportunity to rag on me? Has there been a development in the investigation?"

Seth flopped into his chair. "Nothing so far. But after our chat this morning, I thought I'd come by to see if you asked her out. Everyone is very interested in your progress with Taylor. We voted and decided it was more fun to focus on that than champing at the bit because we can't get involved in solving Mom and Dad's murder."

Shane and his brother shared a moment of reflective silence.

"Everyone?" Shane asked. "What did you do, take a poll?"

"Actually, I did." Seth smiled. "With Sam, Callie and the kids out of the house, we all think it's time you stopped dragging your heels. I swear, Shane, it took less time for Michelangelo to paint the Sistine Chapel, for chrissake."

"He had divine inspiration. I have Taylor's verbal missile defense system. By the way, I know she'd be thrilled to hear my brothers are so concerned about our love life—the one we *don't* have—that they felt it necessary to gossip and send an emissary."

"Whatever," Seth remarked dismissively before taking a long swallow of beer. "So, what's the holdup? How much longer do we all have to stay away?"

"You call this staying away?" Shane flicked a bottle cap at Seth, which he deflected easily. "Besides, what do you care?"

"We're crazy about Taylor, and speaking only for myself, it would be really, really nice if the two of you could hook up before midnight Sunday."

Shane rolled his eyes. His brothers didn't

think anything was off-limits when it came to the friendly placing of wagers. "How much?"

"I bet fifty bucks that you'd admit your undying love before the vernal equinox. Make it happen and I'll split the booty with you."

"Maybe," Shane hedged. "What's the pot up to?"

"Twelve hundred. But only because we made Chandler pony up a thousand on the sixty day over-under."

Shane gave an exaggerated sigh. "Maybe I should work a deal with Chandler then."

"Before you get too chummy with him, you should know he bet the over, that it would take you *more* than sixty days to convince Taylor to accept your sorry ass."

"He might be right," Shane admitted, shoulders slumping under the weight of knowing that he wasn't exactly on the road to success. Forget the road, he hadn't even left the driveway. That could change, if he could come up with a feasible plan. Until he had one, a switch of topic seemed like a good idea. "How are Savannah and the kids?"

"Savannah is hot and my children are cuter, smarter and growing faster than everyone else's."

Shane smiled, knowing full well Seth's remark was part jest and part fatherly pride.

"Speaking with complete impartiality, I'm sure."

His brother stood and launched the now-empty bottle in a perfect arc into the trash can. "A three-pointer."

"Not from that distance, girlie-man," Shane scoffed, tossing his beer bottle behind his back, around his waist, and watching it sail easily into the recycling bin with a satisfying clink. "Now, that is a three-pointer. I am the king."

"Yeah," Seth chuckled softly. "The *lonely* king."

"That was harsh." True, but harsh nonetheless.

"Buck up, bro. I'd be happy to give you some pointers if—"

Shane glared his older brother into silence. "Don't you have someplace to be?"

"Yep. Here." Seth paused and replaced his Stetson, which bore the official seal of the city of Jasper. "I'm checking on a couple of parolees you hired for the calving season."

"Anyone I should keep an eye on?"

Seth shook his head. "One did six months of an eight-month stint for bouncing checks, and the other guy's out on early release on a simple use and possession." Seth glanced at a small pad he pulled from his breast pocket. "Brian

Meyer is the bad-check passer. Luke Adams is the bad driver with the bad habit. He wasn't bright enough to keep under the speed limit while he was rolling a joint on his thigh."

"Don't have to be bright to be a criminal," Shane said with an expelled breath. "I'll keep an eye on them. Thanks for the heads-up."

Seth scanned the notepad again. "I ran checks on both guys when Will sent me their names. Nothing popped in the system. I would've called if anything came up. Meyer is a first-timer, so it's worth giving him a chance. Adams has a few other busts, petty stuff. Shouldn't be a problem."

Shane shrugged. "Will's pretty good at screening them. He wouldn't hire on anyone he didn't think was a safe bet."

"I agree," Seth said. "Still, I want both of them to know I'm in the area. I'll run out to the barn and just say hi before I head home."

Shane walked with his brother to the front door. A rush of cold air filtered in and he was distracted for a minute, wondering if Taylor was dressed warmly enough. Of course not. She'd rushed out without a coat.

"Show them your gun and be sure to look mean," Shane teased.

"Good tip, thanks." Seth raised one hand and

bounded down the steps two at a time. "You have fun tonight! All alone and wandering through the house like a—"

Shane slammed the door, not interested in taking any more of his brother's ribbing. It wasn't like he was ready to concede that his hands-off policy was getting harder and harder to maintain. In addition to his staggering fear of rejection, the truth was the growing intensity of his feelings for Taylor scared him. Keeping her at arm's length was a lot easier than risking everything.

Except that his patience was running out. He felt as if his life had been one big hourglass for the last five years. Finding his parents, after wondering where they were and why they'd left, gave him an odd feeling, a kind of warning bell that there might only be a few grains of sand left.

"She's going to graduate," he told himself as he wandered back into the living room and flopped down on the leather sofa, grabbing the remote control. "Get a job and leave." The thought depressed the hell out of him.

He flicked through the satellite menu without really seeing the images. They had two hundred fifty channels, but there was nothing on. Instead, his mind played visions of Taylor. In the kitchen. Working in the yard. She was as much a part of the Lucky 7 as he was now. Thinking about her impending and inevitable departure weighed heavily on him.

Four hours and fifty-six minutes later, Shane tried again to convince himself that he wasn't actually waiting up for her. *Right?* his conscience ridiculed in a taunting little voice that was irritating as hell. Had to be that he was totally engrossed in the infomercial for the miracle herb that promised everything from increased energy to improved sexual function. Plus, if he acted now, he could get a six-month supply for the value price of only three hundred twenty-nine dollars and ninety-five cents. A veritable steal.

"Like I *need* anything for sexual function," he muttered, standing up and taking his dishes into the kitchen. "My plumbing works just fine, thank you very much. *That* isn't my problem. Sell me a magic pill to read her mind. Now *that* would be freaking worth three hundred and ninety-whatever dollars! Hell, I'd pay ten times that."

He had just put a plate with crumbs of her delicious apple pie in the sink and was about to call it a night when he heard the muffled sound of footsteps on the front porch.

A sense of excitement rushed through him as

he stilled, listening to the door opening and closing, followed by the familiar rhythm of her moving in his direction.

Taylor's subtle perfume entered the room a split second before she appeared.

He knew something was wrong the second he saw her. "Fail a pop quiz or something?" he asked, disturbed by the tension in her hazel eyes.

Damn it. Taylor had hoped he'd be asleep by the time she got home from class. She wasn't up to a verbal sparring match with Shane tonight, she really wasn't. She'd been on a razor's edge through the entire class, absorbing nothing. Anger over the knife and the note had claimed her focus for hours.

Somebody had strolled up to her car, in full view of the house, and had taken the time to open the door, stab the knife and note into her upholstery and walk away.

Who? And why make such a cruel and false accusation about a man who'd just buried his parents?

She tossed her purse on the foyer table by rote, then panicked a little—what if Shane suddenly ripped into it and demanded to know why she was carrying a knife? She shook with pent-up rage, and rubbed her arms as a diversion, trying to avoid him when he stepped farther into the hallway. "Not now, please? It's late. I'm tired." And spitting mad and…

She'd pivoted, fully intending to hide in the sanctuary of her room, when she felt his large fingers gently close on her shoulder. Fighting the urge to lean into the invitation of his touch, she stopped in her tracks. Finding the note, trying to figure out who might have sent it, sitting though a class without processing so much as a word of the lecture—all of it had zapped her energy. She was exhausted and wired all at once—that jittery, caffeine-rush kind of energy that had her stomach burning and her pulse pounding in her temples.

"What's up, Taylor?" he asked softly, the teasing tone gone from his voice.

She opened her mouth, then went mute when he eased up behind her and began to softly massage away the tension that had been holding her hostage since leaving the ranch. His fingers moved gently, subtly. Because her still-damp hair was up in the clip, she was able to feel the warm wash of his breath against her neck.

"Your shoulders feel like rocks. Come on, tell Dr. Shane all about it."

Tell the truth? Lie? She didn't know. Couldn't know, not when his touch scrambled her already taxed brain. The bombardment of sensations easily overshadowed all rational and intelligent thought. It was impossible for her to process anything beyond the soothingly familiar scent of his cologne as he continued the massage.

Warnings flashed in her mind and she couldn't ignore them. Deliberately, she turned slowly, lifting her eyes to his. Taylor noted a slight amount of apprehension in his gaze. But mostly she saw a smoldering, tightly leashed passion that threatened to turn her knees to jelly.

It was easier—not to mention smarter—to simply walk away before this went down the proverbial path of no return. That was the wise move and she knew it. Which was why she lifted her palms and placed them against his chest. She fully intended to push him away, toss out a cutting barb, then find sanctuary in her room.

Those good intentions pretty much evaporated the minute she felt the taut plane of corded muscle beneath her palms. The rapid, even pace of his heartbeat. Shane's body was as solid as a statue and as unyielding as his clear blue eyes. Her fingers fanned out, as if acting of their own volition. Her normally sharp intellect was no match for the years of curiosity that fueled the longing building in the core of her being.

The pads of his fingertips slipped slowly up, over the flushed skin of her throat. His eyes fixed on her mouth, on the way her pale, rose-tinted lips parted ever so slightly when his thumbs hooked beneath her chin. Her eyes blazed but she didn't look away. Brave Taylor. Maddening Taylor. Shane wasn't sure if that was good or bad.

He also wasn't sure what his next move should be. Or even *if* there should be a next move. She sent out mixed signals, and Shane was afraid if he read them wrong he'd be in a world of hurt. He had no idea if Taylor would verbally knock him into the next county or if he was actually seeing possibility in her steady gaze. The signals she was sending right now all seemed to indicate she was as interested and inquisitive as he was. However, she'd shot him down enough times that he was unwilling to rely on the reading or misreadings of signals alone.

"Is now a good time for me to kiss you senseless?" he asked, applying subtle pressure to properly position her upturned face.

"That would certainly level the playing field. Then we could both be senseless."

He smiled in spite of the remark, only because he felt her trembling. Though Taylor couldn't keep her sharp tongue in check, neither could she keep her body from reacting. Thankfully, that much she couldn't hide. The knowledge made him feel a tad more confident. So Shane inched his forefinger toward her mouth. He loved seeing that flash of heat in her eyes as he brushed it across her lower lip. He felt her breath rush over his hand. When she moved fractionally closer, Shane increased the pressure of his fingertip, his confidence rising.

His palm rested against her throat, allowing him to feel a hint of her response. Taylor's pulse quickened, growing more and more rapid as he dipped his head, stopping just short of making contact.

He could have pulled her against him. Lord knew he wanted to—had for what seemed like forever. He could have kissed her, tested the passion that was smoldering in her eyes. But then he would have given up *this*. The heady, powerful sense of expectation coiled in every last one of his cells.

Somehow, seeking personal fulfillment suddenly didn't seem as important as knowing she felt something. Maybe the same things he did. As strange as it sounded to his desire-addled brain, he needed her to make the move, be the aggressor. Say it out loud, clearly, without equivocation, letting him know this was what she wanted from him.

"Tell me," he prompted. "Tell me what you want."

For the first time ever, he saw something bordering on indecision pass through her pretty eyes. Not exactly encouraging, but not totally *dis*couraging either. He took it as a minor victory.

"I—I'm not sure."

It took all of Shane's fortitude and self-restraint to step back. His body practically throbbed with need denied, but if he had any hope of changing the nature of their relationship, this was the best way to go. He hoped. "Well, until you are, I can't help you. Good night, Taylor."

She blinked up at him, said nothing, then turned and walked briskly down the hall. At first, he labeled her quick retreat as a defeat, but then he saw the way she was digging her nails into her palms as she hurried away. He smiled. So, Taylor Reese wasn't as immune as she pretended. That knowledge alone made the whole self-denial thing worth it.

Chapter Four

"You can't be serious!" Taylor stared at the burly detective standing in the foyer. "A search warrant? To find what, exactly?"

"Read the warrant, honey."

Her eyes narrowed as she glared at the man. She didn't care that he had a dozen officers in tow. Nor was she terribly impressed by the shiny gold shield clipped to the front pocket of his tweed jacket. She didn't even care that him calling her "honey" was both demeaning and dismissive and normally would have caused her to launch into a strict lecture on sexism. All of that paled badly in comparison to the dread that came in a rush.

Detective Rollins and his uniformed minions invaded the house. Unfolding the paper, she carefully read the unfamiliar wording, pausing to absorb the part about probable cause. "An anonymous tip?" she repeated.

"Yes, ma'am," the detective acknowledged. "Please stay out of the way during the search."

"Wait until I call Shane. Or the sheriff."

"Call whoever you want." He shrugged. "However, the warrant doesn't require us to wait while you do."

Damndamndamn! Taylor raced for the phone, dialing Shane's cell phone. One, two, three rings, then voice mail. "Wrong time to be ignoring your phone," she said through gritted teeth as she punched in a 9-1-1 page. Next, she dialed Seth, who was, according to his secretary, in court.

Over the din of several simultaneous conversations and the violating sound of drawers being opened and closed, she opted to try Clayton.

"Justice Project."

Relief washed over her when she heard his voice. "Thank God," she breathed, explaining what was happening. "What should I do?"

"First, calm down," Clayton counseled. "Then read me the warrant."

She struggled to keep the emotion out of her voice. The first portion cited the date and time of the tip and identified the officer taking the call. Taylor swallowed, then continued, "The caller directed officers to the Lucky 7 Ranch, primary residence of the deceased. Caller identified Shane Landry as the perpetrator and claimed there was evidence contained in said residence, specifically .38-caliber ammunition matching the ammunition used in the crime."

"Okay. There's nothing to worry about, Taylor, because that's the most ridiculous claim I've ever heard. Shane would never have killed our parents. Yes, there's always been ammunition on the ranch but it's locked up in the attic."

Her blood ran cold. "The attic?" she repeated, lowering her voice to a near whisper.

"Yes," Clayton said. "My dad was big on gun safety. He didn't want any accidents, so the ammo has always been kept separate from the guns. My parents were fanatical about it."

"Clayton, I—"

"Stop worrying," he interrupted. "Everyone in Jasper knew about the house ammo rules. I remember hearing people rag on my dad when I was a kid. Folks used to say it defeated the point of having a gun when you had no way to load it in a hurry."

"Stop!" she insisted, fairly yelling to get his attention. It worked.

"Sorry. What is it?"

Taylor's eyes darted around to find, much to her utter frustration, that several of the officers were openly eavesdropping on her conversation—such as it was. Chief among them was the lead detective, who was standing a few feet away, rummaging through the top drawer of the highboy. "This isn't right," she hedged.

"Trust me on this."

She took the cordless phone and walked out the front door, hardly noticing the cold despite her bare feet. She let Clayton drone on while she wandered out of earshot.

"...sure it is just someone hoping to collect the reward we've offered for information leading to an arrest. The state police are probably inundated with tips. Rollins has to follow up on them, it's his job. And..." Clayton paused and expelled a loud breath "...this is a high profile case, Taylor. The governor and a U.S. senator attended the funeral. Rollins is probably getting a lot of heat on this one."

Taylor felt confident it was safe to talk when she was a good ten yards from the house. "Quiet," she snapped, her nerves frazzled. "Listen to me. I got a note. It basically said the same thing."

"When?" Clayton's tone registered instant alarm.

After telling him about the note and the knife, Taylor asked, "What should I do?"

"Where are they now?"

"In my purse, in the hall. Why?"

"Go back in the house. Do it now."

"I am," she said, briskly retracing her steps. "Then what?"

"Grab your purse and keys and go."

"Where?"

"Anywhere," Clayton answered. "Just get the hell out of there. Do you have a cell?"

"Yes, but shouldn't someone be here while they're going through the house?"

"Technically, no one has to be present. Beside, I'll handle that. You just get out of there. Call me as soon as you're off the ranch."

Motivated by fear and an intense desire to protect Shane, Taylor walked back inside and nearly groaned when she found Rollins still planted in the foyer. How was she supposed to get her purse with its damning contents, with him standing right there?

Oh hell, it didn't matter. She put the phone back on the cradle, slapped the warrant on the table and in precise, clipped syllables, said, "Excuse me."

"Yes?"

"No," she corrected. "I wasn't asking a question, I want you to move."

One bushy brow arched almost accusingly above a penetrating brown eye. "Because?"

"I don't have to be here to watch while you harass this family."

"This family?" he repeated, new interest flaring in his eyes. "I was under the impression that you were an employee."

"I—I am. A very loyal one. One that will go screaming to the press if you and your goons don't leave this home exactly as you found it when you're finished with your little fishing expedition. So, hand me my purse and I'll be on my way."

He did as she asked.

Taylor's heart was pounding as she spun and walked toward the door. She had taken two steps when Detective Rollins said, "Miss Reese?"

She stopped. So did her heart and her ability to breathe. Rollins obviously must have figured something was up. Why wouldn't he? He hadn't impressed her as a stupid man. Stupid, no. Wrong? Definitely.

That didn't change the fact that she was caught. She actually entertained the notion of pulling out the note and eating it. Not smart, but better than giving this man more evidence to bolster the flawed theory that Shane was somehow involved or responsible for the murder of his parents.

Taylor didn't trust herself not to do something rash, making it impossible for her to turn back to face the detective. Her shoulders tensed as she managed to get a single word past the lump in her throat. "What?"

"You shouldn't leave."

Her eyes squeezed shut. "Am I under arrest?"

"Um, no."

She whirled around then, trying to read his expression. No such luck. "Then why can't I leave?"

He pointed at her feet. "No shoes. Unless you make a habit of going out barefoot."

Pressing her lips together, Taylor stiffly went to her room and slipped on some flats, keeping a tight hold on her purse. Obviously, she wasn't suited for a life of crime. Not if her shaking hands and wobbly knees were any indication.

It felt like a lifetime passed before she was tucked behind the wheel of her car, speeding down the long drive toward the main highway. Once she cleared the iron archway that bore the ranch's logo, she fumbled in her purse for her phone and called Clayton back.

"What now?"

"Do you know the old Hudson place?" he asked.

"Kind of."

"Head northeast once you pass through town. It's about ten miles up on the righthand side.

Park by the tanning shed and one of us will meet you there. Can you do that?"

"Sure. There's just one problem."

"What?"

"Which way is northeast?"

SHANE HAD WORKED HIMSELF into an almost blinding fury by the time he shoved open the back door. He just didn't know which thing to be pissed about first.

Detective Rollins won, mostly because he was seated in the kitchen as if he had some sort of God-given right to be there.

In my *house. Thinking* I *was involved in the deaths of my parents.* Shane saw red and stuffed his hands into his back pockets just in case he couldn't contain the very real urge to punch the guy.

"Mr. Landry," the detective acknowledged, not bothering to stand as he continued to flip through a file Shane immediately recognized. Thanks to their mother, each brother had a thick box filled with childhood mementos. Shane suspected she'd done it just to make sure each of them felt special. It was her way of acknowledging each of her boys as an individual. Priscilla had always sworn that someday they'd all thank her for her efforts. It stung to know he'd never have the chance.

Shane felt a poignant, visceral pain at the sight of the familiar handwriting on the side of the box lying open at the detective's feet. His dad used to tease his mom about her appalling handwriting—said it looked as though a fly had fallen into the ink and crawled across the page.

Ah, man… To his heart and mind his mom hadn't died fifteen years ago, but two weeks ago, and he still felt raw.

Seeing that box anywhere near this guy who apparently thought he was guilty of parenticide made Shane's eyeballs throb. Without letting the detective get further than a greeting, Shane glared down at him. "You're way off base."

"Maybe," the officer said with a shrug. "You weren't a very good student, were you, Shane? You don't mind if I call you Shane, do you?"

"Yes, you can call me Shane, and no, I wasn't a great student. But since you're looking at my old report cards, you already know that."

"Have a seat," Rollins suggested, his tone revealing nothing. "We need to talk about a few things."

Reluctantly, Shane yanked out his customary chair and joined the detective at the table.

"You think I killed my parents because I got bad grades?"

"I wanted to give you an opportunity to talk. Clear up a few things."

"Like?" Shane was eyeing the man cautiously. Clayton had warned him not to speak to the cops, but Shane failed to see the harm. After all, he hadn't done anything. Well, nothing *illegal*.

Rollins closed the file, laced his stubby fingers together and rested them on top of the table. "Why would someone accuse you of the murders?"

"I have no idea. The reward, maybe?"

The detective nodded, then flipped open a small notebook. "Tell me what you remember about that night fifteen years ago."

"I wasn't here that night," Shane reminded him, annoyed that he was being asked to repeat facts he knew full well were part of the missing-persons report filed fifteen years earlier. "I moved out that day."

"What precipitated the move?"

Shane kept his gaze level, while his heartbeat faltered. "It was time," he said easily. "I was eighteen."

"You stayed away for five years. Why was that?"

"I wanted some space. Out on my own. I can give you a list of the ranches I worked during that period, and there are any number of people who will vouch for me."

An uncomfortable silence stretched out before Rollin sighed pensively and asked, "How come a guy whose family owns one of the biggest spreads in western Montana runs off to work as a hired hand for someone else?"

"That's the reason," Shane answered confidently.

"Why **be** the help when you can be the boss? I don't get that. Someone wanted to hand me a ranch on a silver platter, you better believe I wouldn't up and decide to do grunt work."

"I'm not sure why this is such a tough concept for you to grasp." Shane felt a whole slew of unpleasant memories churning in his stomach. "I wasn't the boss. My father was. As far as I knew, he'd continue to be the boss, so the fact that I left should be enough to convince you that I couldn't possibly have been involved."

"That's certainly one way to look at it."

Anger washed over Shane as he again was treated to an noncommittal response from the detective. "It's the only way."

"Okay." Rollins stood with a grunt, started toward the door, then glanced back. "I should ask, Shane, how did you get on with your parents?"

Guilt assaulted him. "Like any eighteen-year-old."

"Could you be a little more specific? Good, bad, what?"

Shane's mind played a series of video clips. Happy memories interspersed with some that weren't so happy. Then the chilling details of that last time he'd seen his parents alive. "More like okay. I was a pretty volatile kid. And stubborn. A lot like my father, actually."

"Really?" Rollins pried. "How so?"

Meeting the man's gaze, Shane answered, "He taught me not to suffer fools gladly. Is there anything else?"

"Not right now. Maybe when I get results back on the items we're taking. One of the officers should be in with an inventory for you to sign."

"Whatever."

"I'm sure we'll be talking again soon, Shane."

Defiantly, Shane replied, "I'll be right here."

He was right there ten minutes later when the phone rang. Shoving aside the promised inventory sheet, he grabbed the receiver with such force he sent the base unit sailing across the counter. "Landry."

"Shane!" Taylor wailed into the phone. "Are you okay? Are the police still there?"

"They're gone. But forget about the police. A note? A knife? What the hell were you thinking, Taylor? And why didn't you say anything?"

"I don't believe this! You're yelling at me?" she huffed as she raked her fingers through her hair. Hair that was blowing all over the place. Because she was outside. In the cold. With no coat. In the middle of blasted nowhere. Smelling whatever possibly toxic chemicals were leeching from the metal drums littered everywhere. Saving his butt. "You ungrateful jerk!"

"Don't even go there," he warned, his bellowed words echoing in her ear. "Details, Taylor. Right now, before Seth gets there. I don't want to hear them secondhand. Not like I had to hear from Clayton about the note and knife you got. How could you keep something like that from me?"

She was so angry she wanted to scream. Instead, she very childishly hung up on him, and in an even more childish move, she went over to a nearby, rusted-out barrel and kicked it. Hard. Which accomplished two things: her toe hurt and she had an ugly scuff on one of her favorite shoes.

When her cell phone vibrated as it played Beethoven's *Fifth,* she purposefully waited to answer until the last possible second before it switched over to her voice mail. She started to pace on the rutted surface of the unattended driveway. "Maybe I did the wrong thing, but I did it for the right reason," she declared before Shane could say a single word. "You owe me an apology."

"No, you owe me one, Taylor."

She stopped short, recognizing the muffled voice from yesterday, when she'd been baking pies. Man? Probably. Woman? Maybe. Creepy? Definitely.

"This is not a good time, either," she snapped, wishing now she'd spent the extra three dollars a month for caller ID from her cell service.

"Pay attention, Taylor. How do you think I got this number?"

She rolled her eyes. "Off the Internet, no doubt. Not exactly a challenge in this day and age. This really isn't a good time, so—"

"Look to your left."

Annoyance gave way instantly to the rush of fear, making the hairs at the back of her neck stand on end. *Don't be stupid,* she told herself, yet she couldn't help but turn her eyes in that direction.

Nothing. Nothing but an empty field with the remnants of a stripped pickup and a few more barrels. How dare this little weasel pull a B-horror-movie thing? She was equally annoyed at herself for buying into the prank.

"I looked. Now will you get off my phone?"

She was about to hang up when the caller asked, "Do you see the truck?"

Okay, she was completely terrified now. She spun in dizzying circles. "Uh-huh." She didn't see anyone. Nothing but the rustling trees far off in the distance. How could he know where she was? Hell's bells! No one knew. No one that wasn't a Landry.

Maybe it was just a lucky guess. Yes. Good! Had to be it. The wind was strong, easily letting the person on the other end know she was outside. The truck? Also easily explained. Virtually everyone in Montana had a truck. This was just like those fake psychics. They listen, pick up audible and visual clues, then tell you what you want to hear. A cute parlor trick, but not now.

"Great, there's a truck nearby. Are we finished?"

"Keep watching the truck, Taylor, and remember, it could just as well have been you. Get him to confess. If he runs, I'll find him. If you run, I'll kill you. Then he'll have your blood on his hands, too."

"What in the—"

Pop.

It took a second for her eyes to pick up the cause of the sound. The truck rocked. She frowned. What...? The windshield of the old truck spiderwebbed. It took several seconds for the sound and the image to register in her frozen brain.

Her breath left her lungs in a rush of sheer, unadulterated fear. Someone had shot the truck.

Chapter Five

"Are you sure you're okay, honey?" Shane asked for the fifth time since she'd been practically carried into the house.

Taylor was numb. The adrenaline rush she'd experienced in the field at the old Hudson place had faded, leaving her feeling spent and heavy. Until her brain processed the fact that he'd called her "honey," something Shane never did. He wasn't about casual endearments.

"I'm fine," she insisted, willing it to be true. "I'm sure the caller just wanted to freak me out and, well, he…she…*it* succeeded."

Shane maintained a tight grip on her hands as he knelt in front of where she sat on the edge of the living room sofa. He examined her with his piercing eyes, the troubled lines etched on his face not relaxing until he'd apparently satisfied himself that she had not been injured in any way.

She glanced around, listening to the quiet of the house, then asked, "Where's Seth?"

"Went to his office," Shane replied. "He's going to see if he can track the calls or the knife."

"Shouldn't we turn that stuff over to the state police?"

He scowled. "Eventually. I'm not trying to hinder the investigation, I just need to do whatever I can to find out why someone wants people to think I killed my parents."

"How did it go with Detective Rollins?" she asked. Shane looked troubled—no, more than that, haunted, bordering on tormented. Seeing him this way tugged at her heart. Taylor slipped her hands free, placing one flat against his cheek. His dark head leaned into her touch and she heard him expel a slow breath.

Briefly, he closed his eyes, feeling some of the tension drain away after seeing for himself that she was safe. When he'd heard someone had taken a shot at her, his heart had literally stopped. "Rollins is impossible to read," he said, distracted by the faint traces of perfume she'd dabbed at the pulse point on her wrist. "I have a bad feeling I'll know soon, though. This is pretty sick déjà vu. I always thought I knew how Clayton felt when he became a suspect in Pam's murder. Believe me, it's ten times worse when you're the target."

"Maybe you're reading too much into it, Shane," she said as her small fingers caressed his cheek.

"Maybe," he agreed. Her simple gesture was both soothing and exciting. Best of all, it served as an important reminder that there was something more pressing at hand. "We've got to get you packed."

"Didn't you hear what I said?" she asked, jumping up so fast she very nearly had him toppling back on his heels. "The caller was very, very specific. Neither one of us can run."

"Seth and I talked about that and we agreed that—"

Anger flashed in her eyes. "I don't care what the two of you *agreed.* I'm not willing to risk your life."

Shane used the time it took to get to his feet to consider the possible implications of her statement. The caller's threat against Taylor had been specific and lethal, yet her argument was all about what might happen to him. What, exactly, did she mean? he wondered, confounded. Was it some sort of coded way she was admitting she had feelings for him? Or was it nothing more than Taylor being a stand-up person caught in a situation that was out of her control? Maybe he should ask.

Right. He could just hear himself now: *Taylor, are you saying you're willing to die for me?*

Ah, hell. She wouldn't just think he was a moron. She'd know it.

He lifted his head to find her standing in the center of the room, hands on her hips, fiery challenge in her eyes. If things weren't so dire, he would have been amused by her display of stubbornness. While he appreciated the power of her conviction, he also knew she was no match should the caller decide to get up close and personal with her. She had to go, so he told her as much.

"No. This is nonnegotiable, Shane."

"You're in danger."

She sent him a castigating look. "I don't believe that."

He felt anger flare in his gut. "Weren't convinced by someone shooting at you? Christ, Taylor, what more does it take?"

"That's my point," she countered. "I was a sitting duck. Outside, isolated—a perfect target. If the...*whoever* wanted to kill me, it would have happened right then and there. It didn't, and I'd bet that's because I'm not really the target. You are."

He ground his teeth until his jaw hurt. "If I believe every word you just said—which I don't—but if I did, that's sufficient reason to send you packing. Ever hear of collateral damage? I'm not willing to risk your safety. It's not an option. Get packing."

"Get real," she retorted. "You may not like it, Shane, but I'm in this now. I fully intend to see it through."

"Why?"

That single word seemed to shake her in a way none of his earlier arguments had.

"B-because! That's what friends do for each other."

He closed the space between them in two long strides. "Is that what we are? Friends?" Holding his breath, he hoped her answer was no. Hoped she just might give him a hint to how she felt.

"Of course." she took a step back and folded her arms in front of her. "You…irritate me, Shane, but I won't let that get in the way of things. Besides, where could I possibly be safer than in among all you Landrys?"

Hardly the admission of undying love he longed to hear. Okay, forget undying love; he'd happily take a hint that she felt some affection. Lord, he was starting to seem desperate and pathetic even to himself.

Seth was right. Shane was his own worst

enemy. If he had any hope of winning her over, he needed to take the bull by the horns. He should probably start by not thinking in terms of lame clichés.

"Okay. There is some merit to your argument."

"My arguments always have merit. Haven't you figured that out in the last five years?"

Most of the tension seemed to drain from his body when he heard the humor she'd purposefully injected into her tone. "Your arguments occasionally have merit."

She scoffed before smiling up at him. "Your life would be much easier if you simply embraced the fact that I'm always right," she teased.

"In this instance—and only this instance—you might be. He could have killed you in the field but didn't."

Taylor spread her arms as if about to take a theatrical bow. "Thank you for acknowledging my superior skills of deduction. But we don't know it is a he."

"Okay, *it*," he said with an exasperated breath. "Whatever. You can stay. With conditions."

"There really isn't any need for conditions." Taylor's tone no longer had that sharp, combative edge. She braced herself, half expecting him to tell her she would be locked in her bedroom for the duration.

"Wrong," he exclaimed, his voice firm and unyielding, as were his eyes. "No more trips out to deserted fields. Or deserted anythings, for that matter. Stick close to the ranch. If you have to go out, I go with you. If I'm busy, I'll arrange for one of the hands to go. But under no circumstances—I am serious about this, Taylor—are you to leave here without protection. Understood?"

She responded with a salute. "Sir, yes, sir."

"It's getting late." He took her hand and led her from the room. "Why don't you take a relaxing bath and I'll rummage around for dinner."

Taylor tried not to think about the little shocks of electric current pulsing where his hand held hers. It was a losing battle from the get-go. She noticed everything—the calluses on his palms, the strength in his tapered fingers. Her thoughts were so distracting that she nearly stumbled as she walked a half step behind him.

Great, the guy holds my hand and I forget how to walk. Not good. Not a raging endorsement for my mental fortitude. She wanted to believe that her insistence on sticking her neck out for him was a simple tribute to her decency as a human being.

Even later, when she was drawing the bathwater, she refused to wander into the danger-ous territory of the truth. It was simpler to examine the motivations of others than it was to turn the tables on herself. Particularly when it came to her feelings for Shane.

Stripping off her clothing, she slipped into the hot, soothing water. Maybe she could wash them away. Scrub off the feelings she wouldn't acknowledge, but couldn't explore. Doing so would derail her life plan.

She rested her head against the pillow at the back of the tub, letting the warm water massage her body. Though her muscles were relaxing, her brain was not.

The threatening situation offered the perfect excuse to leave. "That's what I want, right? So why didn't I take the easy out?" she asked in a whisper.

Her own words echoed off the tiled walls, almost taunting her for the answer. "Because when all is said and done, regardless of my careful planning, regardless of my education or my degrees, I'm *her.* I'm living proof that life's bad choices are cyclical. I could have left. I should have left. I had an out but instead argued to stay. Insisted! Knowing it is the worst possible choice. Knowing it is not in my best interests. Knowing it is flaming *dangerous.* I am," she acknowledged as she started to lower herself below the waterline, "a complete idiot and very much my mother's daughter."

TAYLOR TOOK HER TIME primping, dressing, basically dragging her heels. It was never easy to admit you were on the road to heartache. "Yet here I am," she sighed as she pulled on some thick socks. Out of habit, she spritzed on perfume and fluffed her hair before venturing out.

The house smelled of bacon, and that brought an instant smile to her lips. Shane's culinary skills were limited to scrambled eggs or BLTs.

She stopped in the hallway, realizing he hadn't heard her approach. A thrilling sensation started in her belly, then spread the tingle all through her body. Shane was busy assembling sandwiches. An innocent, normal activity that was anything but.

The sleeves of his denim shirt were rolled to midforearm, but it was the way the fabric hugged his broad back and shoulders that drew her interest. Well, that and the way his worn, faded jeans outlined his narrow waist, great butt and long, powerful legs. Taylor actually shivered.

That initial tingle morphed into warmth, making her feel flushed all over. The man inspired any number of fantasies—vivid, needy desires that only made the hot flash worse.

So, of course, he had to turn around at that moment. Turn and see the unguarded passion that must have been evident on her face.

It was. He did.

At least she assumed so, since he tossed the knife on the counter and virtually issued an invitation with his gaze. Tension crackled in the air between them. Tension born and raised on years of denial.

It would be so easy, not to mention satisfying, to simply walk into his arms. Easy but stupid. She had to remember that.

Swallowing hard, she cleared her throat and said, "Smells good."

His head tilted, and she could almost hear the litany of questions racing through his mind. Questions she couldn't answer.

"Want me to set the table?" she asked as she breezed in, heading for the drawer with every intention of getting silverware.

Shane was having no part of it. Not this time. Not after seeing the hunger in her eyes. "No." For once, he was confident when he reached for her. "Not after the look you just gave me."

He caught her by the waist and pulled her against him. Her soft curves fit him perfectly.

Her hair smelled of citrusy shampoo, a scent complementing her subtle, feminine perfume.

She peered up at him through her lashes as her palm flattened against his chest. The fluttery sensation of her fingers splayed on his body caused his heart to skip a beat.

Shane spread his feet as he placed his other arm around her. It allowed him to compensate for their height difference, but offered the added bonus of settling her snugly against that part of his body that ached and throbbed.

"You feel good," he murmured, pressing his lips to her forehead.

Her breaths, shallow and unsteady, tickled his throat. Taylor's hands were trapped against his chest. Her fingers closed, grabbing fistfuls of his shirt as she leaned into him.

Her back arched slightly as she lifted her mouth to his. Shane countered, leaning back to study every beautiful inch of her face. He smiled, moving his hands up her back, deliberately counting each vertebra until his fingers tangled in her silken hair. "Ready to ask yet?"

She blinked. "Ask?" she repeated in a husky, painfully sexy tone he hardly recognized. "Why do you think I'm standing here?"

He slipped his thumbs beneath her chin, feeling the racing pulse at her throat. "That's the problem, Taylor. I never know what you think. So I need to hear the words from you. I want to know that you need me."

Stunned was the only word he could think of to describe the way he felt when she practically rocketed out of his hold. How did they go from passionate embrace to this?

"What?"

She moved back, until she was practically plastered against the wall. Nervously, she fidgeted with her hair and kept her gaze averted. And she hadn't answered. He took a step toward where she stood.

"C'mon, Taylor, we—" He was silenced by the fact that she went rigid, looking…frightened. "I don't get this," he admitted. "You walked in here all hot and bothered. Don't try to deny it, either. I saw the look in your eyes, Taylor. I felt the way you trembled in my arms. And the next thing I know, you're cowering in the corner. What gives?"

She rubbed her face, sucking in a deep breath. "It's complicated, Shane."

"Try me," he suggested, moving back to lean against the counter. It gave him something to do with his hands, something other than shaking her until she opened up.

"I don't want to start something I can't finish."

"More like you don't want to start something *period*. Why? It's because you don't think I'm your intellectual equal, right?"

"Where did you get that stupid idea?" she demanded in a pretty convincing imitation of surprise.

He wasn't buying it. "You are always making cracks about it. Just because I don't have—"

"A clue." She fired the retort at him. "My apprehensions have nothing to do with your IQ. How could you even think such a thing?"

"Because you tease me mercilessly?" he suggested.

"I tease you because it's easier."

"Easier than what?"

She met and held his eyes. "Easier than any of the other options."

"You're wrong."

"No," she said, her shoulders slumping. "It could never work between us."

"That remains to be seen."

"What does that mean?" she asked, her brow wrinkled.

"It means," he said, as he walked over and tapped the tip of her cute little nose, "that I'll have to work hard to change your mind."

Chapter Six

Taylor's restless night was ten percent delayed reaction to the scary experience at the abandoned Hudson place and ninety percent reaction to Shane's comment.

Or maybe it was more like two percent to ninety-eight percent. At any rate, it was bad. So, as had become her practice since moving to the ranch, she needed to work out her frustrations by doing something in the kitchen.

Luckily, Shane's room was on the second floor, insulated from any noise. Shane's room—the one with the huge four-poster bed and masculine appointments. Taylor didn't want to count how many times she'd pressed his pillow to her face when changing his sheets, just to smell the heady fragrance of his skin. Or how many times she'd uncapped his cologne, or lain on his bed and fantasized about how different things could be—

"Stop it," she snapped as she flipped on the switch. The reality was if she wanted sex with Shane all she'd ever had to do was *ask*. As she well knew, a man didn't have to be emotionally involved with a woman to have sex. And she'd made her decision about casual sex years and years ago. Long before she'd ever met Shane Landry.

Sex with him would be... Taylor pressed a hand to the butterflies dive-bombing in her tummy. Sex with Shane would be incredible. She knew that. Just having his mouth on hers was enough to fry all her brain cells and make her forget her promise to herself.

Never depend on a man to make you happy. She mouthed the words to herself. Reminded herself that her mother had been tempted, too. Many times. And look how well that had turned out for her mom every time she ended up caved in like a wet meringue.

"No thanks, not me." Taylor Reese was going to use the excellent brain God had given her, and parlay it into a satisfying, lucrative career. She was going to get personal satisfaction helping people who needed her. She was not—absolutely *not*—going to throw her life and happiness away on the whim of a man.

Not even a man like Shane Landry.

No matter how strong the temptation.

And, heaven help her, his attraction was overwhelmingly strong.

"Idiot." Dawn was still hours away, but she couldn't lie in bed, staring at the ceiling, for another second. So she'd tugged on her sweats, her socks, and pulled her hair into a ponytail, opting to do something mindless yet constructive.

The kitchen was cold but spotless. Shane was good about that. He never left a mess. Not even when she'd rushed through the meal he'd prepared and raced to her bedroom like the chicken she was.

She was still frowning at the thought a few minutes later when the coffeepot coughed and sputtered, signaling it was done. Taylor poured herself a mug, warming her hands on the cup as she pondered her baking possibilities.

Deciding on what cookie to make was less complicated than trying to figure out what, if anything, to do about Shane. Or more accurately, what to do about her feelings for him.

"Which are?" she asked. Redundant question. She knew how she felt about him. She'd just gotten really adept at burying those feelings deep inside. So adept, in fact, that having them gurgle to the surface was hard to handle.

Feelings that were locked away deep in her heart or laid out raw weren't really the issue. The real problem was knowing she couldn't do anything about them. Not if she wanted to break the ugly pattern that had defined and destroyed the previous three generations of Reese women.

By the time she finished her cup of coffee, Taylor had decided to make peanut butter cookies. Going to the walk-in pantry, she nearly tripped over a box someone—Rollins's search warrant team, most likely—had shoved inside.

Irritation rose in her throat, so fervently that she could actually taste her own anger when she thought about the detective and his ridiculous suspicions. Personal vexation aside, she was instantly curious when she saw the scrawled label affixed to the box. Just a name—"Shane."

Yes, she knew it was wrong to look. It could be full of private things that were none of her business. Knowing all that didn't seem to stop her from plopping down on the floor and lifting the lid. She justified her inappropriate prying by telling herself she was only checking to see if it contained anything that might exonerate Shane as a suspect in the murder of his parents. That was a good thing. It would get the police and the creepy caller off their backs.

"I'm a regular saint for doing this," she muttered, knowing full well her ability to rationalize her behavior didn't make it right.

The box, she realized as she scanned the neatly labeled compartments, was very personal and very organized. Hanging tabs created color-coded sections. Nestled inside each divider was a collection of folders organizing every aspect of Shane's life. There were crisp certificates of accomplishments covering everything from T-Ball participation to science fair ribbons. Yellowed, wrinkled school records were lined up in perfect chronological order.

Taylor couldn't resist the temptation, especially now that she knew he was so touchy about his intellect. Which was, she knew, absurd. How could he think he wasn't smart? Didn't he get that she understood what it took to run this place? Apparently not.

She pulled the school section out and placed it in her lap. She hesitated for a moment, reminded again that she had absolutely no right to pry. She wasn't prying; she was helping.

"Liar," she whispered as she opened the file. She smiled as she read, in great detail, Shane's less-than-stellar years in the Jasper School District. Apparently the man had never mastered the fine art of working and playing well with others. Several of his teachers noted a propensity for "independent thought"—educator code for refusing to do work as assigned.

There was a fat section devoted to invitations for conferences with the principal of Jasper High. Said principal's last few letters included discussions that caught Taylor's attention instantly. Apparently there was some concern about Shane's well-being and safety. His defiant attitude coupled with reports of frequent bruising had been red flags to the teachers.

"Was Caleb Landry abusive?" she wondered aloud, hearing her words echo in the room. That was something she'd never considered, but it would certainly explain a lot. Especially why Shane had bolted from the ranch once he turned eighteen, and then stayed away for so long.

It also might explain the haunted look in Shane's eyes whenever his father's name was mentioned.

Licking her fingertip, she quickly flipped through the file, trying to find some sort of comment, response or something to indicate his parents had reacted to the subtle but dire accusations from the principal. She didn't find anything indicating there had been a resolution.

After carefully replacing the file exactly

where she'd found it, Taylor braced her hands behind her and leaned back to ponder this new information. Although she'd never heard a whisper that Caleb Landry had been a violent man, Shane's school records indicated that that might very well have been the case. This knowledge was a double-edged sword. If true, it would explain a lot about Shane's motivation for leaving the ranch, but it was also a strong motive for murder. She wondered if the school had ever contacted the authorities. Probably not; child abuse was considered a private family matter back then.

"What are you doing?" Shane asked from the doorway. Taylor gave a guilty start. No wonder. She *was* guilty. "I—I was cleaning the pantry," she stammered, pulling the prop of a dust cloth off her shoulder.

"You did that last week. How dirty does a pantry get?" he asked. His gaze flickered to the box on the floor as soon as he stepped into the room.

Shane leaned his large body against the wall and held out his hand, helping her to her feet.

"Boning up on my life history?" he queried.

A haunted look was present in the deep lines etched on his face. Compassion quickly erased her guilt as she looked at the man and, for the first time, saw the possibility of a childhood that wasn't as idyllic as she'd always been led to believe.

"I couldn't help it. You know me," she managed to murmur over the lump of emotion in her throat. "I'm not very good at minding my own business."

He offered a small smile before rubbing his hands over his face. "Rollins was going through that box when I got here yesterday. I'm not sure why, though."

"That doesn't automatically mean something bad." The pantry was small. Very, very small when filled with six feet of sleepy-eyed Shane Landry.

He cast her a sidelong glance. "I'll say again, I'm not stupid."

There was such pain behind his statement that she felt like she had to do something. "Let's get out of here, I'm getting claustrophobia." She followed him back into the kitchen, nudging him to sit down in his chair as she poured him some coffee. Kneeling in front of him, Taylor closed one hand over his and reached out to cup his cheek in the other. "I do not think you're stupid. I never have and I never will," she said forcefully, holding his gaze.

Shane leaned forward and rested his forehead against her shoulder. She heard him sigh deeply as his face turned. His breath fanned against her throat as she stroked his head. She intended it as a comforting gesture. A harmless display of empathy for a man who'd probably spent a lot of time in deep, private emotional pain. She understood that very well. She also knew full well that child abuse led to desperate thoughts, which led to desperate acts. She didn't want to consider the possibility, but...

"I have a bad feeling about this. Rollins didn't say so, but I'm pretty sure he thinks I killed my parents."

She should have been thinking only of supporting him, but she wasn't. She was thinking about the fact that his hands were at her waist. His fingers separated, the tips nearly touching her spine. Here he was, in the midst of a personal crisis, and she was cataloging the scent of soap clinging to him, the even sound of his breathing and the firm muscles beneath her touch.

As she mentally damned herself to the fires of hell, Taylor started to inch out of his grasp. Shane resisted.

"Just let me hold you for a minute," he said in a voice she barely recognized. "Please?"

She couldn't very well say no to something she so desperately wanted herself. "Everything will work out," she promised, massaging the tight knots at the base of his skull.

"I don't think so." His pain-filled voice was muffled and her heart constricted. *Oh, Shane...*

Taylor focused off into space, silently pleading with her conscience to stop berating her as she stroked the back of his head. "There's nothing to worry about yet, Shane. Think positive thoughts until you have a solid reason to think otherwise."

"You don't understand, Taylor." His voice broke. "I *do* know otherwise. Fifteen years ago, I did something terrible."

"What?" Taylor asked, capturing his face in her hands, steeled for what he might admit. "What did you do?"

He read a thousand fleeting emotions in the pretty hazel eyes trained on his face. But it was the trust he saw in them that stabbed at him like a knife. She was going to despise him if he told her the truth. She was going to know what a jerk he'd been.

He was the first to look away. "I can't tell you, Taylor."

"Sure you can," she insisted, her palms cool on his skin as she exerted enough pressure to force him to look at her again. Her gaze was un-wavering. "Believe me," she said softly, her thumb brushing against his cheek. "No good ever comes of keeping secrets."

Her fervent tone gave him pause. Regarding her quietly, he felt as if he was looking at a total stranger. A *dangerous* total stranger. Was this Taylor Reese, almost-psychotherapist, speaking? Or Taylor Reese, fantasy woman who didn't want to get too close to him, showing concern?

It could only be his imagination that made her words sound as though she knew from bitter experience what keeping secrets could do to a person. Which was absurd, because Taylor was the most straightforward, least secretive person he'd ever met.

As if life wasn't complicated enough. The day had barely started and already it was turning into a pretty intense cruel fest.

"Talk to me, Shane. Whatever you did, I'm sure it was justified. I'm sure the courts would take that into consideration and—"

"Courts?"

"If it was self-defense?" she prompted.

Stunned, he looked into her eyes as he gently set her aside. "You think I killed my own parents?"

She twisted a lock of pale hair around one finger. "There are situations, Shane. Circumstances when—"

"Jeez, Taylor!" he bellowed. "I said I did something terrible, not criminal. Don't you know me better than that?"

"We can never *really* know another person. I know you're a good man, Shane. So does everyone in Jasper. Whatever happened in the past can be fixed."

"No," he countered, "it can't." He raked his hair back off his face, incredulous that she would even entertain such a thought. "I didn't kill anyone, for chrissake."

He stood and went to the sink, looking out the window briefly before saying, "That last night, I, um, had a fight with my father."

She scrambled up and moved to the far side of the room, pacing, rolling her hands one over the other, perhaps in time with her brain. "And you exchanged words. One thing led to another. You struggled and maybe he fell and hit his head and—"

"Hey, Oliver Stone?" He would have laughed if the whole scenario wasn't so close to the truth. Well, all but the last little part. "Yes, I had a fight with my father. Yes, it got a little physical. But I was the one who ended up on my ass, not vice versa."

She paused and glanced in his direction, then went back to her pacing ritual. "Okay. So you knew your father was capable of physical violence. So…later on, fearing another altercation, you acted in a preemptive fashion to—"

"Earth to Taylor!" he called, moving over to take her by the shoulders in order to guide her to a seat at the table. "Since I'd like to stop you from trying, convicting and sentencing me, I'll tell you what happened. But first you've got to swear you won't repeat this story."

She blinked rapidly. "Wait! Maybe you shouldn't say anything. Remember what happened with Clayton and Tory? If I'm called to testify, I wouldn't have a choice."

"I'm willing to take that risk," he countered, mirroring her solemn expression even though he found himself perversely amused by her overreaction. So amused, in fact, that he lowered his voice to a conspiratorial tone and added, "If it does come to that, we can get married because, as we all learned, a wife can't testify against her husband."

Her eyes grew wide. "Okay," she agreed on a rush of breath.

He wasn't so amused anymore.

She bobbed her head as the words fell quickly from her lips. "We could do that if need be. All right. That's settled. Go ahead, you can tell me what happened."

"You'd marry me?"

"I wouldn't send you to jail," she answered. "We could use the subterfuge to fend off any court proceedings until we can figure out a way to get you off. Or…" she continued, folding her hands neatly in her lap, as if they were agreeing on the final preparations for a barbecue "…your lawyer negotiates a plea bargain."

"Or you could remember that you have a triple digit IQ and listen to me for a minute."

Her mouth snapped shut.

It was his turn to pace. Shane wasn't sure where to start. He just knew that with the investigation focusing on him, he had to tell someone. "I walked into the kitchen that night with a boulder-size chip on my shoulder. I was itching for a fight."

Taylor watched him take ten steps, turn and take an equal number in the opposite direction before repeating the pattern. Watching him wear an invisible rut into the floor allowed her to avoid thinking about the fact that in less than ten minutes, she had agreed to marry him as part of a defense strategy. *Where did that come from?* "Remind me again. How old were you?"

"Just turned eighteen," he said, his gaze focused off in the distance. "Thought I knew everything, too."

"Common adolescent mind-set."

He shrugged. "I guess."

The action pulled the well-washed cotton shirt taut against his shoulders. Taylor swallowed her errant thoughts. "So, you went into the kitchen and…?"

"I was hot and tired and pissed because he'd had me digging the new well by myself for the third straight day."

"Hard job. But necessary." Cruel of Caleb. Digging a well was backbreaking work for a team of men. What kind of vicious father would force his own son to do it alone? "The old well is the one where the…bodies were recovered?"

"Yes." Shane took in a deep breath and expelled it slowly. "Dad found out I'd broken the pump on the old well. Not from me, mind you," he admitted with more than a touch of guilt. "Which was why, instead of letting me fix the pump, he had me digging a whole new well."

"A character-building exercise," she murmured, thinking it wasn't a bad idea. The discipline seemed appropriate for the infraction. So, Caleb wasn't quite as big a creep as she'd first thought.

"I think he asked if I was finished yet, and my response was to tell him to go to hell."

"Not a good choice, huh?"

Shane rolled his eyes and sighed heavily. "He was furious. He jumped up and took a step toward me. I held up my hand, aiming for his chest, but somehow I managed to catch him in the nose. It bled, and the next thing I knew he had knocked me flat on my back."

"This? This is your terrible thing?" she asked. "You smarted off to your father. Then he raised his hand to you. That is *never* acceptable."

Shane shot her a glance. "Maybe not in perfect-parenting land. Get real, Taylor. I had height, muscle, age and attitude on him. Believe me, I deserved to be taken down a notch. Should have ended there, but it didn't." His expression grew dark.

She braced herself for the confession. "You were provoked."

"I was a teenager with a bruised ego," he snapped. "I decided to share some of that pain, so I lashed out."

"Understandable."

"I said some nasty things, Taylor. Really nasty. I guess I had stored up a lot of frustration and I just let loose."

"It happens."

"Not like that," he promised, joining her at

the table and taking her hands in his. "I told him I was embarrassed to be his son. That was one of the kinder things I said."

"Shane..." she murmured, knowing full well there was little she could do to assuage the anguish in his eyes.

"It got ugly," he admitted, sadness making his voice heavy. "Mom came in, there was a big, dramatic scene. And—and..."

"What?"

Slowly, his eyes lifted and met hers. "I threatened to leave. Tossed it right there on the kitchen floor like a gauntlet. Flat-out dared him to try and run the ranch without me."

"Hoping he would be sobered at the thought of losing you and tell you how valuable you were to him and the family, and the argument would end?" she guessed.

He squeezed her hands. "Maybe. I don't know. Yeah. Probably."

"But?"

"He gave me an hour to pack up and get out."

Taylor cringed, just imagining the scene in her head. "So being a hardheaded eighteen-year-old, you left?"

"Yep. Took years for me to get the anger out of my system. Until I was finally ready to come back and patch things up with him."

But you never got the chance, she thought, her heart aching. "It was a fight. Nothing more. Why do you think that was so terrible?"

"While I was packing, I heard my parents going at it. Big time." He yanked back his hands, stood and returned to his pacing. "She was begging him to reconsider. He was accusing her of favoritism. I couldn't hear it all, but I did hear her accuse him of taking his anger out on me instead of her. Which made sense, since for the week leading up to the fight, my dad had been a real bear. There was something going on between the two of them. One minute they'd be holding each other, the next minute my father was ranting and raving."

"So they were in a rocky place. That happens in some marriages. Sounds like she was trying to get him to rethink the situation."

"Well, it didn't do any good. He yelled something back at her I couldn't hear. I stormed out of the house." Shane sat and dropped his head into his hands. "The last words I said to my father were said in anger. Now I know I can't ever make that right."

She scooted close to him, grabbing his hands. "Don't do this."

"I can't help it," he admitted, his expression

and his tone dark. "I'd give anything if I could live that night over again. What if I hadn't been such a jerk, Taylor? They might not be dead."

Taylor pressed each of his palms to her mouth, kissing them in turn. "You can't know that, Shane."

"Easy for you to say. You didn't destroy your whole family."

"Now see? There you go again," she said. "Thinking you're the center of the universe. You aren't, Shane." Her hand lingered on his face. "A boy had a fight with his father. That's all. What your parents did afterward had nothing to do with you. It sounds to me as if you were a cocky kid who happened to find yourself on the edges of an ongoing argument between your parents. Hardly your fault. And rather conceited of you to think that you alone were capable of preventing a double murder, don't you see that?"

He reached up and took her palm from his face, kissing her fingers. "All that fancy education of yours is really paying off, isn't it?"

"It doesn't take a psychologist to see that this has been hurting you for fifteen years."

His guilt and pain started to fade as he reached to frame her face in his hands. "Will you kiss me better?" he asked, his voice husky as he urged her face closer to his.

"I'm offering support and all you can think of is kissing?"

"I'm game if you are."

She wanted his mouth on hers, Taylor admitted to herself, closing her eyes. Wanted to feel the warm brush of his breath on her lips, the firm pressure of his fingers tunneling through her hair.

When he tugged and brought her to him, taking her in his arms, she felt so many things all at once. The primal, womanly part of her knew kissing Shane was everything she'd ever wanted. Her rational side warned against such a foolhardy move; passion always trumped reason. Especially when every one of her senses was under the heady spell of having Shane's body pressed against her own.

Taylor memorized everything—the way his thighs brushed hers; the way his palms flattened against her back, fingertips splayed.

The need to mold her mouth against his, to finally have that first taste, was fierce and consuming. It dominated all of her thoughts and burned in her belly. She'd gone far beyond wanting it, she needed it. Soon. Now. Her body's sole reason for existing was the promise of the kiss to come. The culmination of years of vivid fantasies was at hand.

Lacing her fingers behind his neck, she pulled gently but urgently. Feeling his resistance, she met his hooded gaze. "What?"

"Savoring the moment," he said, his voice so deep and sensual it sent a thrill though her. "In a hurry?" One dark brow arched as his mouth curved into a sexy half smile.

"Actually, yes."

His warm lips brushed her forehead, igniting all the cells and adding unnecessary fuel to the embers sparking in her stomach. Breathing normally wasn't an option. Not when her whole body was little more than a cauldron of simmering need.

This had never happened with anyone. This consuming desire that pulsed, deafeningly loud, in her ears. Taylor felt as if she were under siege from every one of her nerve endings. She was on fire and he had yet to kiss her. It didn't seem plausible that the anticipation alone should have her quaking all over.

She tugged more forcefully, moving her body against his in hopes of ending the wait.

He moaned softly against her skin—a low, soft growl that made her feel powerful and feminine all at the same time. It was a heady sensation. One that fed the current electrifying the room.

The sudden sound of the phone ringing made her jerk away from him, completely shattering the moment.

"Hold that thought," Shane told her, his eyes giving her a promise as he leaned over to reach the insistently ringing phone on the counter. "It's got to be one of my brothers. They're the only ones who would dare call here so late. I swear, there are times when I hate Alexander Graham Bell for inventing this thing." He slapped a button on the base unit, putting the call on Speaker as he kept one arm firmly wrapped around her waist. "Shane Landry."

"Put Taylor on the line."

He frowned at the brusqueness of the command. "She's a little busy right now, since it's barely dawn. Try calling back at a decent hour." Though his tone was harsh, it was tempered when he winked playfully in her direction.

"You're running out of time, Shane."

Taylor's blood stilled in her veins as she recognized the threatening, angry voice.

"Who is this?" Shane demanded.

"You need to confess. You have one week. Do it or she'll die."

"Hey, pal," Shane warned in a cold, merciless tone. "I don't know what—"

With a loud bang, the line went dead.

Chapter Seven

"That's it," Shane announced, "you're getting out of here. I'll get you on a plane and—"

"Wait!" Taylor pressed the heels of her hands against her eyes. "We have a week."

His jaw dropped for a second. "You actually trust a person who took a shot at you to keep their word?"

She nodded. "Sure, and it isn't like we have a lot of choices here. So let's figure out how to make the best use of the time we have." Taylor opened a drawer and grabbed the pad of paper she kept for grocery lists, pulled a pen out of the cup on the counter and went to the table.

Shane's lips twitched. "We're going to solve my parents' murder using a pad of paper in the shape of a kitten?"

She ignored his little taunt. "The first call I got said the evidence was in the attic." She looked into his eyes and asked, "Does that mean anything to you? Anything jump out?"

"The only time I go up in the attic is to get ammunition or holiday decorations."

"The ammo," she said as she scribbled a note. "What about the box in the pantry? Where did that come from?"

"The attic. Rollins brought it down," Shane said with a tad more enthusiasm. "Hang on." He hurried out of the room and reappeared a minute later with a sheet of paper. "This is the inventory of stuff they took after the search."

He placed it on the table, allowing them to review it together. "The gun case, one box of old bank statements and a family photo album," Shane murmured. "The box and the case were in the attic. The photo album was in the office. I'm not seeing a pattern here."

"Forget what they took," she said. "Let's focus on the things they left behind."

"Such as?"

"Well…" she hesitated as she went to the pantry "…maybe Rollins missed something."

Shane came and got the box and placed it on the table. "You want school, medical or athletic?" he asked.

"Your call," she answered, taking the stack of files he handed her and settling into the chair.

While Shane thumbed through his stack, Taylor opened the file marked Medical and silently prayed something would jump out at her. Some magic fact that would reveal the identity of the killer. However, she learned nothing from the first few pages other than Priscilla Landry had made certain her youngest child was immunized on schedule.

Nothing but common childhood illnesses, not until the age of five. "You had the mumps?" she asked, trying to decipher the handwriting at the bottom of the receipt from the doctor's office.

"No." Shane took the paper out of her hand, a smile curving his lips. "Wrong Landry," he mused. "Look at the date. This was before I was born, so the 'S. Landry' listed as the patient was Sam, not me. He never actually had the mumps. As the story goes, several of the hands had mumps and my mother was terrified that one of her boys had been exposed to the disease. I think she dragged him into the doctor's office every day for two weeks.

"Must have just been misfiled." Shane patted Taylor's hand. "God's way of punishing her for having so many sons with names that start with the same consonant."

"It is confounding to us outsiders," Taylor

joked, hoping her voice sounded even because her heart rate certainly wasn't. Nope, not with his finger making those maddening circles on her skin.

A few minutes later, she came across another weird receipt in the file. "What's a platelet function test and why did you have one when you were ten?" she asked.

Setting aside the riding ribbon he'd been holding, Shane looked at the paper. "I remember that," he mused, frowning. "My mom drove me all the way to Helena to some lab. Then she bought me ice cream, a Fleetwood Mac album and a very cool die cast model of a red Gran Torino like the one in *Starsky and Hutch*."

"So—" Taylor grinned "—you were a butter-fat-craving car freak with a thing for Stevie Nicks?"

"Pretty much." Shane stroked his chin for a second. "Gotta give me points for great taste. Stevie Nicks is still one fine looking woman and that Torino was a hot car."

"You were obviously a man ahead of his time." She snatched her hand out from under his. "But you don't remember why you were having tests?"

"I was ten," he reminded her with a small chuckle. "All I remember is that it hurt. Why?"

"Well—" Taylor pressed her lips together as she considered ways to broach such a touchy subject with him. "I saw some notes from teachers. Maybe your mother was…*concerned*."

"Not that again," he groaned. "I was not a battered child."

"But you just told me you and your father had a physical altercation," she reasoned, hoping it might make him more willing to open up to her. "Was it a pattern of behavior?"

"It was an eighteen-year-old kid getting what he deserved," Shane insisted. "Didn't your father ever put you in your place?"

"No."

It was the way she said the single syllable that caught his attention. Not sad, not angry, just flat. No effect, no emotion and not at all Taylorlike. "What's that about?"

"What?"

He scratched his head and scooted his chair at an angle so he could better see her face. "Come to think about it, what is your family situation?"

"We only have a week, Shane. Let's concentrate on this stuff before we go up to the attic."

"Oh, no you don't," he countered, tipping her head up with one finger and forcing her to look at him. "We can spare a few minutes.

You're sitting here pawing through the first eighteen years of my life, so I think it's only right for you to have to share a few personal facts about yourself."

She fidgeted in the chair, something he'd never seen her do before. It only made him more determined to extract a few details. He also knew one of her few weaknesses: she could be guilted into things, because at her core, Taylor was a people pleaser. All people but him.

But that was about to change. He was not going to let her walk out that door without at least trying. Not yet. "I told you about the fight I had with my dad. Something I never told any other living, breathing soul. I confided in you." He was on a roll now. One that was working if her pinched expression was any indication. "I entrusted my secrets to you. Now I feel like—"

"Okay," she huffed, shoving her hair off her face with a vengeance. "Just remember, you asked to hear this tawdry tale."

"I did," he agreed, placing his hand on her knee, giving it a squeeze, then leaving it there as he looked into her troubled eyes. "I do."

"After giving birth to me, my mother left the hospital and went directly to a lawyer's office to file a paternity suit against the married man who was my father."

"Sounds like she was just looking out for your best interests," he offered.

"I don't think *I* entered into the equation. See, I was the means to an end. She wanted that man. The man who didn't have any desire to leave his wife, so I was the trap. A way for her to get what she wanted."

"Whoops." Shane flinched. "People make mistakes."

"That was just the first one in a long line of mistakes," she told him bitterly. "Since Mom's plan backfired, we had no choice but to move in with my grandmother, who was, at the time I was born, the ripe old age of thirty-six." One pale, perfect brow arched as she watched him do the math. "Yes, sir, my grandmother did almost the same thing. However, her lover wasn't married, he was selected as her ticket out of the house. That lasted less than two years.

"My grandmother wasn't too thrilled to have us around, so my mother set her sights on one loser after another. None of my 'uncles…'" she paused to make air quotes, "…lasted very long. She'd fall in love. We'd move to wherever uncle du jour could find work. The relationship would spiral, normally ending with blowouts that required police intervention. I think I learned how to spell 'restraining order' before my own name."

"Oh, Taylor…"

"We're not finished yet," she insisted. "When I was ten, my mother hooked up with a guy fresh out of jail. Duane Treadwell was a nasty drunk and my mother, for some sick reason, worshiped him."

"Did he hurt you?"

"Me?" Taylor repeated. "Heavens no. Duane barely noticed I was in the house. Probably helped that I spent most of my time burrowed under the covers with a book and a flashlight. They lived together for about three months when it happened the first time. It was a school night—I remember because my science project was on the kitchen table. One of those volcanoes every kid has to make?"

Shane nodded, remembering it well. "My lava didn't bubble when I added the vinegar."

"I heard screaming and thuds. More screaming and then a loud crash, so I went running out of my room."

"And?"

"Duane was straddling my mother, pounding her already bloody face. I ran to the neighbor's house—I'm not sure either one of them heard me leave—and called the police."

"I hope they locked the bastard up."

She shook her head. "Mom wouldn't press charges. So after spending half the night in the back seat of a patrol car, I ended up going back inside to find that during their fight, my volcano had been smashed to pieces."

"What about your mother?"

Taylor shrugged. "The paramedics patched her up. One of them, a nice red-headed guy, kept urging her to go to the hospital, but she wouldn't leave Duane."

"I'm sorry, Taylor," Shane exclaimed.

"Well, everyone has baggage. The police officers who responded that night alerted Family Protective Services. I was pulled out of class the next week. The caseworker tried to convince my mother to voluntarily remove me from the home. She was more than willing."

"That *really* sucks." Shane felt his body tense as he imagined the scene.

"So, off to Grandmother's I went, only she was in pretty much the same situation. Her boyfriend at the time would disappear for days on end, return smelling like cheap perfume—I'm not sure how, but he had a second woman supporting his sorry butt. He and Grandma would fight, more police. Never any charges filed, just more begging and pleading and empty promises, yada, yada, yada.

"I was shuffled back and forth depending on who had the lesser-evil man in her life at the time. Until I was thirteen."

"What happened then?"

"My mother had spent three whole months without Duane. A record, by the way. It was the first time ever, I think, I'd made it through a whole half year without changing schools. She got a job as a cocktail waitress in some dive outside the town were we lived. That's how I learned how to cook," Taylor added as an aside.

It was the only time during the story that Shane had seen a hint of anything other than pain in her eyes. "For which I am eternally grateful," he declared fervently.

"Thank you. Then one night she came in and I heard her laughing, so I knew she wasn't alone. I figured it was some guy from the bar. My mother always had her eye out for the next man she was sure would make her life whole.

"It took a minute, but I eventually recognized the voice. Duane was back. I remember sitting in my room, feeling physically ill when I realized he was back in our lives. Mom was ecstatic, welcoming him back as if all the beatings and broken bones were an acceptable price to pay for a prize like him."

"Maybe we should drop it," Shane suggested, feeling all kinds of horrible for making her relive everything.

"Why? Don't you want to know how the story ends?"

"I'm guessing not too well," he said, taking her hand in his and pressing it to his lips.

"No, not well at all. Mom quit her job so she could be home at Duane's beck and call. It wasn't long before he slipped back into the same predictable pattern of all my mother's boyfriends. He'd be charming, then snap. They'd fight, she'd forgive him."

"Duane was a pig," Shane said, holding her hand to his cheek.

"But it was *her* choice," Taylor argued fervently. "She was defined by the Duanes in her life. She didn't make a single decision in her entire lifetime that wasn't predicated on finding a man, keeping a man or pleasing a man. Even me. The only reason she had me was to try to bond herself to a man who never really wanted her in the first place."

"We don't get to choose our relatives."

Taylor smiled at him, which seemed to ease

some of the torment he read in her eyes. "No, we don't. You got very lucky. I got Duane."

Curiosity got the better of Shane. "What happened to him?"

"He died."

"When?"

"A hour after he killed my mother."

Shane grimaced and squeezed her hand. "You were thirteen?"

Taylor nodded slowly, stiffly. "Yep."

"I'm assuming you went to live with your grandmother?"

"You'd be wrong," she said, pulling her hand free. "My grandmother had just met the new man of her dreams, and taking in her teenage granddaughter wasn't tops on her list of priorities. Since my mother had never identified my biological father, I went into foster care."

"That's rough."

Taylor chuckled softly. "It should be," she admitted, "but in truth, it was the best thing that ever happened to me. I lived with three families over the course of five years. When you're in the foster care system, you know everything is temporary, but I was used to that. It took me longer to adjust to family dynamics that didn't include fighting and hitting and police and…"

"What happened to your grandmother?" Shane asked.

"Last I heard, she was in Arizona living with a guy she claimed was her one true love. That was seven years ago."

Shane regarded her for a long time. "I'm really sorry for you, Taylor. No kid should grow up feeling scared and unloved."

"Like you said, we don't get to choose our relatives." She gave his arm a gentle squeeze. "Don't look so horrified, Shane. I dealt with my grief and losses a long time ago. I'm over it."

"Is that why you don't have relationships?"

"I have relationships." Her fingers fell away from his arm. "I date, Shane. More often than you, by my count."

"Yes, you date," he conceded. "But not for very long. Name the last guy you went out with more than three times."

She opened her mouth, and he grinned when she had no choice but to snap it shut. "See?"

"Don't act so superior, Shane. Ever think I might just be waiting for the right guy to come along?"

"Nope," he answered confidently. "After hearing your story, I'm pretty sure that you wouldn't recognize the right guy if he had it tattooed on his forehead." He chuckled. "You're not aloof, Taylor, you're afraid."

"Hardly," she said. "I'm just not going to be like my mother and my grandmother. I'm not ever going to let myself *need* a man."

Chapter Eight

"I'm going up to the attic," she told him, annoyed at him, at herself—hell, even the sun slipping over the distant mountains was getting on her nerves. *Why did I have to go tell him all that personal stuff?*

"I'm coming, too," he said, his mouth curved in a wide grin.

That didn't improve her sour mood. Not when she replayed his snide little "tattooed" remark in her mind. Didn't he get it? Obviously not, or he wouldn't have been so quick to...*to hit the nail on the head?*

Taylor was chased out of the room by her inner turmoil. Someone had taken a shot at her; Shane topped a short list of murder suspects. So this was a pretty bad time to be rethinking her life plan just now.

With him on her heels, she climbed the staircase to the second floor. The fading scent of lemon oil filled her nostrils as her hand skimmed the polished banister on the way up. Except for hers, all the bedrooms were on the second floor. She often tried to pick a favorite. Not an easy chore, since each room had its own unique feel.

With the parents' bodies found, she wondered if the master suite would be redone. It hadn't been touched since their disappearance, save for dusting and vacuuming, in all these years.

It was a gorgeous room, with handcrafted furniture custom-made for the space. Decor included a rich, warm palette of corals and beiges that worked perfectly with the greens and browns of vegetation visible through the large window that dominated one wall. A beautiful stone fireplace was angled in one corner, allowing whoever was on the bed to see not only a flicker of a warm fire, but also the majestic Rockies beyond.

The bathroom was massive, but it was the only one in the house that hadn't been redone. Taylor could practically close her eyes and imagine the possibilities of a complete makeover. Polished granite vanities, updated fixtures, maybe even a walk-through shower. *Or maybe I should stop decorating a room I won't be here long enough to see!*

Accompanied by Shane, she continued down

the long hallway toward the attic ladder, automatically using her sleeve to erase a palm print on the hall table as she passed. Rollins or his men, she guessed, frowning. "You should do something with these rooms," she told Shane as they passed the empty bedrooms vacated months earlier when Sam and his family had moved to their new home.

"What do you suggest?" he asked.

"Furniture would be a good start."

"Not my area," he countered, reaching around her to capture the string dangling from the ceiling at the end of the long hall. "I like to think I'm a sensitive guy, but I draw the line at fabric swatches and paint chips. You should do it."

"I can't." She backed up as he unfolded the hinged ladder that allowed access to the attic.

"Why not?"

"First, it's not my house," she said, turning and lifting her face to his. "Secondly, to do it correctly, I'd need more than four weeks when my schedule is already crazy. Even if I didn't have a threatening caller running me in circles, I have final exams to take, résumés to send out, packing…"

His expression darkened as he reached and grabbed her around the waist. He lifted her onto the second step, magically erasing the height differential.

A curious thrill danced through her when she found herself eye to eye with him for the first time ever. His head tilted ever so slightly and that sexy, crooked half smile of his ignited a little fire in the pit of her belly.

"We need to be investigating in the attic."

"Even Nancy Drew took some personal time," he countered, tucking a wayward lock of hair behind her ear.

"If you're going to confess to being a closet Nancy Drew fan now, it will really spoil the moment for me," Taylor teased, feeling the tension build in the inches separating his mouth from hers.

"Well, I have no intention of spoiling the moment," Shane said, his deep voice resonating all the way into her bones. "Kiss me, Taylor." His fingers lingered, stroking her cheek.

Curiosity that had been with her for years took on a new character—one she could only define as raw, powerful, urgent need. Taylor searched his face, somehow accepting that something between them had changed.

Shane saw the transformation in her. It was subtle to be sure, but he recognized it instantly, instinctively. Days and nights of wanting her fortified him as he placed his palms on the sides of the ladder. "Tell me what you want, Taylor. It has to be your decision."

He rested his forehead against hers, savoring the feminine scent of her flawless, smooth skin. "I don't want to rush you, but I'm not sure how much longer I can keep my hands off you."

Watching her, he swallowed a groan when her tongue darted out to moisten her lower lip. Her mouth glistened in the pale glow of filtered light streaming in from the window.

"Please, Taylor? Tell me what you want, but do it quickly."

"I honestly don't know. I'm all confused and…" Her husky voice trailed off as her palms flattened against his chest.

Shane felt the small tremor in her touch, saw the hint of a smile on her mouth and decided that combination was encouragement enough. Wrapping her in his arms, he held her for a second, reining in his own fierce desire.

Decision made.

Lifting her off the ladder, ignoring her muffled shriek of surprise, he carried her back down the hallway. Preternaturally aware of her every breath, he twined his fingers in her silken hair as he carried her to his room. He relished the feel of her soft form against his chest, vividly aware of the swell of her breasts and the taut flatness of her stomach. His body's response was intense and immediate.

It was nothing shy of a miracle that he found his way to the bedroom, given the passionate fog swirling in his brain. When his shins contacted the edge of the bed, he lowered her to the mattress.

He expected—hell, was braced for—a long and convoluted reason why they shouldn't be doing what they were doing. But none was forthcoming.

Since she wasn't protesting, and hadn't beat him about the head with a blunt instrument, Shane took it as a sign and felt free to breathe again. Laying her in the center of his bed, he slid next to her, placed one of his legs over hers, then searched her upturned face. Her hands began to skim the taut muscles of his back. When her fingertips began exploring the contour of his spine, Shane wasn't sure whether to push or pull. Every one of his greedier, baser instincts longed to surrender to his primitive desires.

His dwindling self-control wanted her begging, wanted there to be no question that her need was as great as his own. As he looked deeply into her eyes, he knew he didn't want her to merely enjoy, he wanted her pleading for his touch, totally sure and totally wild. Desperate even. Maybe then she would see the truth: nothing that felt this right could possibly be wrong.

With that singular goal in mind, he lowered his mouth and began teasing the seam of her lips with his tongue. It took immense willpower to savor the moment while harnessing his own passions in order to inspire hers.

He kissed her softly, angling her face beneath him by gently tugging the strands of her silky hair tangled in his hands. He felt her nails dig into the planes of his back as he slipped his tongue into the warm recesses of her mouth.

Deepening the kiss, Shane dropped one hand to her tiny waist and urged her against him. She complied willingly, even enthusiastically. Having Taylor in his arms, feeling her body against his, inspired a sudden clarity that had nothing to do with lust. He didn't just want her. He loved her.

That should have scared him. Terrified him even, but it didn't. It made him want her all the more.

"You taste like coffee," she said against his mouth. "Shane?"

He held his breath, afraid she'd call a halt to things. Afraid she wouldn't. "You taste better," he said, burying his face against her throat. Her heated skin tasted fresh and clean. No cologne, no perfume, just Taylor. It was a heady, alluring scent.

Taylor could hardly breathe. He was exciting, strong and solid. The weight of his leg fell across her abdomen, pressing against the core of her desire. It was becoming more and more impossible to keep her passion in check. She groaned and lifted her lashes when his mouth trailed a fiery path to her lips. He kissed her again as he shifted in order to work his leg between hers. The intimacy of the action lanced through her, forcing her to arch against him as her primal instincts responded. "Shane," she whispered, knowing full well it was now or never.

He made a strangled, guttural sound that tugged at her resolve. "Don't,' he pleaded as he lifted his dark head. The raw, blatant sensuality in his voice was almost as erotic as the feel of his hand slinking up her rib cage.

His blue eyes locked on hers. "Don't stop me now, Taylor. It will be good," he said as his mouth dipped to her throat. "So good."

"I know," she admitted, clamping her eyes shut. "That's what I'm afraid of."

He caught her face between his hands. She

noted a tremor in his square-tipped fingers. "You're driving me crazy, Taylor. Do you have any idea how much I want you? How long I've wanted you?"

"I think I've got some idea," she teased, arching her body against the unmistakable evidence of his desire.

A deep, rich moan rumbled in the back of his throat. Taylor felt very powerful at that instant. It had a heady effect on her that formed an effective barrier between her conscience and her passion. She'd deal with the consequences of her rash behavior later. For now, she slipped her arms around his neck and drew him to her. Opening her mouth eagerly to his, she banished all doubts in favor of satisfying her own urgent desires.

"Tell me you want me," he instructed in a nearly desperate whisper. "I need to hear the words from you, Taylor."

"I want you."

"Finally," he breathed, as he moved to cover more of her body with his.

Now that he knew exactly what was driving him, Shane hurried to pull the shirt over her head. Much to his pleasure, Taylor was doing some exploring of her own. She had unbuttoned his shirt and splayed her fingers across his chest. She stroked upward, flattening her palms against his nipples.

"You have an amazing body," she breathed admiringly.

Shane thought he might explode with male pride. It was the first time she'd given him a compliment and it did incredible things to his ego.

"As do you," he murmured, propping himself up on his elbow as his fingers made easy work of the front clasp on her lacy wisp of a bra. As he covered one of her breasts with his palm, he noted her skin was pleasantly flushed, and he could feel her heart beating against his hand. When he teased her taut nipple between his thumb and forefinger, she sucked in a quivering breath and his hand stilled. "Did I hurt you?"

"Not exactly," she told him with a wry smile. "Unless it counts for me to admit that I want you so much it aches."

"That counts, honey. Big time," he said, grinning down at her.

"Why aren't you kissing me?" she asked, desperation in her voice.

"I'm watching. I like seeing the way your eyelashes flutter when I do this," he explained, tracing the outline of puckered, mauve skin surrounding the tight bud of her nipple. "Or maybe this." He delighted in hearing her sharp intake of breath when his mouth closed on her body. She went instantly rigid, then arched her back as her hands gripped his head.

Shane made quick work of dispensing with their clothes, then took his time exploring every beautiful inch of her body. She was perfect, exquisite, and reacting to his touch with a primal, greedy honesty that convinced him she, too, felt more than just lust.

When he finally buried himself inside her in one heartfelt thrust, Shane was half out of his mind. It was so perfect, so right. She matched him move for move, as if the encounter had been choreographed. He tried to make it last, wanted this to go on forever. But when he felt her shudder, felt her teeth nip at his shoulder in the throes of climax, it sent him over the brink. He moaned softly, feeling his body shatter as his need spilled into her.

Much, much later, Taylor lay cradled in the crook of his arm, but it wasn't just the two of them there. Nope, she'd been joined by a large, heavy quantity of guilt and remorse and…*son of a gun, was that ever good!*

She had to remind herself that this was just sex. Great sex. Incredible *Shane* sex. But just sex. Not a lifetime commitment.

Good. Great. Perfect.

Exactly the way she wanted it.

I have to make my own way, build my own life. Then and only then, can I even consider sharing any part of myself with someone.

She could keep beating herself up, or she could get up and make sure it never happened again. Everyone was entitled to make a mistake.

Mistake, my foot! her conscience argued. That was some seriously toe-curling, mind-blowing sex.

"We'd better get back on task," she suggested, clutching the sheet to her chest as she grabbed up some of her clothing.

Shane looked over at her, wearing nothing but a lazy, sexy smile that made her blush. "I like this task. Give me five minutes and—ouch!"

She elbowed him, then insisted he hand her the clothes that were out of her reach. "Focus, Landry."

"I'm focused," he assured her, nuzzling her neck.

Taylor's spine melted, but she managed to resist the temptation of spending more time in his bed.

Shane reluctantly got up, handed Taylor her

bra and panties, then pulled on his jeans. He felt better than he had in, well, forever. Acknowledging to himself that he was completely in love with Taylor was the difference. Now, he just had to figure out a way to get her to see the light.

He turned, read the jumbled emotion in her eyes and knew he had his work cut out for him. He shrugged on his shirt, realizing she was uncomfortable at the prospect of dressing in front of him. He swallowed a smile, knowing she wouldn't appreciate the fact that he found that amusing. They'd just shared the most intimate encounter known to mankind and she was reluctant to let him see her naked.

"I'm going to get a drink. Want me to get you some water?"

She nodded.

"Be right back," he said, kissing the tip of her nose.

He went down the stairs whistling, feeling on top of the world. So happy it was everything he could do to keep from puffing out his chest and having a manly Tarzan moment. Another thing he was pretty sure Taylor wouldn't appreciate in the least.

He had just come off the last step when there was a loud knock at the front door. Rolling his eyes, he wondered which of his nosy brothers he'd find on the other side. He also felt lucky that he hadn't bothered to unlock the door earlier, as was his practice. What if one of them had walked in on them? Taylor would have freaked. There was no way he was going to let any of his brothers mess this up. There was too much at stake.

He was going to make winning her heart his mission.

Starting now. By telling whoever was on the other side of the door to buzz off.

Twisting the lock with one hand while simultaneously turning the knob, Shane was surprised and annoyed to find Detective Rollins on his doorstep.

"Yes?"

"May I come in?"

"For what?"

"We need to talk. We can either do it here or at the station."

Shane eyed the man, curious, but also feeling alarm bells sound in his head. "What do we have to talk about that's so important?"

"The DNA results. You were a match to the evidence on the bloody towel found in the well."

"That makes sense, since my understanding is my parents' blood was on that towel."

"It was," Rollins agreed, shifting his weight from foot to foot. "Because we took DNA from you and your brothers, the lab was able to isolate the samples on the towel." Rollins pressed his lips together, then repeated, "I really think we should do this inside, Shane."

"Suit yourself. Come on in." He kept his tone even, but Shane had a bad feeling. That sense of foreboding caused the hairs at the nape of his neck to prickle as he ushered the detective into the living room.

Buttoning his shirt, Shane remained quiet as Rollins selected one of the chairs flanking the sofa, and sat down.

"So," Shane prompted, "what's the problem?"

Rollins pulled out his trusty little notepad. "What do you know about DNA, Shane?"

"Enough to know that people get half of theirs from each parent. Which totally explains why my blood would be a match to the samples. It was, right?"

Rollins nodded. "You and your brothers all matched two out of the three samples."

Shane relaxed, taking a deep breath and letting it out slowly. "So what's the problem?"

"The results showed an…*abnormality*."

"What does that mean?"

"Well, Shane, the lab people tell me you and your brothers should have matched the same samples, since you're siblings."

"We didn't?"

"No," Rollins answered, his voice solemn. "Can you explain that?"

Raking his hands through his hair, Shane considered the possibilities. "Sure. Your lab screwed up."

"Not likely," Rollins said.

"How can you be so sure?" he asked, catching a glimpse of Taylor in his peripheral vision. He motioned her into the room. "You remember Taylor?"

"Yes," Rollins said, getting to his feet and extending his hand in her direction. "Not to be rude, Miss Reese, but I think Shane might prefer if you weren't in the room when—"

He draped his arm around her shoulder. *"Shane,"* he said, jaw tight, "has no problem with her being in the room."

The detective shrugged. "Suit yourself."

"Can I get you something? Coffee?" she asked.

Shane almost laughed. He knew her well—well enough to know there was a lot of hostility buried in that polite offer. "Don't bother. The detective won't be here that long. Detective? You were in the middle of telling me why your lab couldn't possibly have made a mistake?"

"If there was a mistake, then there'd be no way your DNA would match two of the samples."

"But I did match," Shane countered. "Right?"

"Yes. According to the lab, the sample provided by you is a blend matching the DNA identified as that of Priscilla Landry and the unidentified third sample."

"What does that mean?" Taylor practically yelped.

"It means," Rollins explained, "that based on the samples of the seven brothers, the lab was able to identify the bloodstains on the towel as belonging to Mr. and Mrs. Landry as well as blood from another, unrelated individual, probably their killer."

Shane's mind spun at a dizzying speed. "So you're telling me Caleb Landry wasn't my father?"

"That and worse," Taylor said, her large eyes lifted to his. "He's suggesting the DNA results indicate you're the killer. He's saying you killed your parents, Shane."

Chapter Nine

Chance Landry was seated in his customary seat at the family table, his eyes scanning the report for the second time.

"You're a doctor," Taylor practically yelled, "explain what this means."

"It makes no sense," Chance said, deep lines etched on either side of his eyes. "Where's Shane now?"

Taylor angrily blew at a stray hair caught in her lashes. "The detective had a warrant for another blood sample, so Shane had to go to the state police lab."

Chance shook his head, his expression a blend of anger and agony. "Shane *is* a Landry. I don't give a cra—crud what the DNA says. The samples were degraded. That evidence was down a well for fifteen years."

"That's what Rollins said. That's why he wanted another blood sample from Shane."

Taylor felt like a caged animal, and a useless one to boot. "What can I do?" she asked, pacing restlessly.

"He left you here alone?" Seth chimed in after appearing suddenly in the doorway.

She glanced over at him. "He didn't have much of a choice. Besides, I got another call." She spent a few more wasted minutes bringing the brothers up to speed.

"You bought that one-week thing?" Seth scoffed, grabbing the phone, punching the keypad with a tad more force than necessary. "This is Sheriff Landry. I need a rush dump on incoming calls to this number." He ended that call and made another. "Sheriff Landry. Put me through to the bank manager, please."

"What are you doing?" Chance asked.

Seth covered the mouthpiece, then said, "I want copies of the bank records Rollins took. I'm not going to sit around and do nothing."

"Me, either," Chance agreed. "I'll see if I can't track down Shane's old medical records. Maybe there's something in there that can explain this DNA foul-up."

Taylor listened as the brothers mobilized, which was comforting, but did little to assuage her feelings of uselessness. Clayton was called, dispatched to the state police lab to obtain samples for independent testing.

The bank manager would have the copies within the hour, so Seth could deliver them to Sam for review. Chandler's job was to hunt through newspaper archives, pulling any stories written about the disappearance of the Landrys. Cody was all over old police records, using his FBI contacts to see if any similar crimes with the same MO might have been committed around the same time.

"I need something to do," Taylor insisted. "How can I help?"

"By staying put and staying safe," Seth answered. "I asked Will to send one of the hands up here until Shane gets back."

She balled her hands into fists at her sides. "I would prefer something a little more proactive," she complained. "I can't do nothing!"

"Sorry, Taylor," Chance said. "The best thing you could do to help him is to stay here. We have to focus all our efforts on Shane right now."

A scant few minutes later, she was standing alone in the kitchen. That didn't last too long. Luke Adams knocked on the door and she almost didn't remember meeting him. Then she saw the tattoos on his knuckles and the flash of his cosmetically-corrected smile.

"Ma'am," he said in greeting, tipping the brim of his hat before removing it as he came inside. "Will sent me up here to sit with you."

"No need," she countered as politely as possible under the circumstances. "I mean, make yourself at home. I've got some things to take care of upstairs."

His eyes sparkled with interest. This time when he openly checked her out, she found it offensive. "On second thought, why don't you have a cold drink and enjoy the view from the porch." She hurriedly grabbed a can of soda from the fridge, slapped it into his hand and all but shoved him and his hat out the door.

Taylor raced up the stairs, ran to the attic ladder and climbed up into the musty darkness. Her hand ran along the wall until she found the switch and flipped it with the tip of her index finger.

It was a massive space, running almost the entire length of the large home. Taylor frowned when she noted that the boxes were no longer neatly stacked against the wall. Rollins and his warrant cretins had certainly made a mess. As she moved farther into the cavernous space, she cursed the detective, then coughed as her movements kicked up dust.

Taylor's search wasn't exactly a methodical

undertaking, probably because it was her first ever. There had to be in excess of fifty boxes in the attic, in addition to several sealed plastic containers, old furniture and countless accessories and accent pieces.

"I can probably forget the cradles," she mused, distracted as she briefly admired the handcrafted items. The spindles and detail work were familiar; she recognized the same hand that had done much of the woodwork throughout the home. Shane was a direct descendant of the town founder.

"Or so we all thought," she muttered, still confused by the results of the DNA tests. They had to be wrong. A mistake, faulty, something. "A lot like my self-control."

Taylor felt a twinge of conscience, an annoying mix of regret and exhilaration as a memory of her morning tryst with Shane flashed vividly. "Tryst?" That didn't seem at all a fitting description for the explosive passion that still lingered in her system.

Banishing those thoughts for another time, she willed herself to focus on the task at hand. Problem was, she didn't really know what to look for. "Hopefully, it will jump out at me."

The only direction came from following Rollins's lead. She went to the spot on the floor where a ghost in the shape of a four-foot-by-three-foot, dust-free rectangle appeared. "The gun case," she whispered. She glanced around, hoping for inspiration, since the guns were in the custody of the police. She spied a box marked "Hunt Club" and figured there might be some sort of connection between guns and hunting.

"Or I'm just really, *really* desperate," she grumbled as she lifted the lid off the box and looked inside.

Unlike the childhood memory box of Shane's, most of the writing on these files was done in a sweeping, masculine hand. Caleb Landry's, she guessed.

In thirty minutes, she knew a lot more about hunting than she ever wanted to know. Caleb had served two terms as the club's president. She knew because she came across two pictures and a certificate that said as much. More photos were stuffed in an unlabeled file. Judging by the clothing and confirmed by the date stamped on the edge of the picture, they were from some party in June of 1967. Caleb and Priscilla were in all the photographs, some alone, some with other people.

"The year before Shane was born," she murmured as she flipped through the images. "Which means…" she looked away and counted backward "…nothing." Taylor frowned. June 1967 was more than ten months before his birthday, so there was nothing sinister about the pictures.

"Except bad fashion," she joked, taking in the trendy overuse of shimmering blue eye shadow, loud funky prints and frosted white lipstick.

She paused over one photograph, recognizing several of the people. Caleb and Priscilla, of course, but also a much younger Will Hampton, the ranch foreman, posed in the group of eight. She continued to stare at the woman with one arm around Caleb's shoulder. It was a familiar face. It was… "The woman from Webb's Market…Debbie, no, Doris! Doris Tindale," Taylor said aloud. She turned the picture over, hoping someone had noted the names of the other people in the shot.

No such luck, which was frustrating, because the other men were also familiar, she just couldn't place them. Rummaging through the box, she didn't find anything of real interest. Tucking the picture into the pocket of her top, she moved on.

It took another full hour working her way through boxes before she found something that might be significant.

"Date books," she whispered excitedly, dumping them onto the floor. For the first time she was thrilled that the Landrys were such pack rats. Until then, she'd loathed the fact that nothing ever seemed to get tossed out. Now, she was almost giddy to find Priscilla Landry's daily life chronicled year by year inside the pages of the school fund-raiser styled books.

Not just her life, Taylor noted, duly impressed. The lives of every member of Priscilla's family were tracked as well. Taylor discovered such mundane, normal things as Caleb's standing tee-off time, each Sunday at nine. And that Sam spent three years in art lessons in the early seventies.

Taylor opened each book, narrowing her search to the year Shane recalled having the special blood tests. If there was something to the fact that his DNA wasn't wholly Landry, that might explain those tests.

But why wait until he was ten years old? Why do it at all? Unless Priscilla suspected Caleb wasn't Shane's father. Taylor got a chill thinking about it.

Unlike her situation, Shane had grown up with two parents. This might devastate him. Being a Landry was part and parcel of his identity.

Taylor thought of her own father in unflattering terms—as a sperm donor, nothing more. It wasn't as though she'd ever missed something she'd never had.

But Shane was different. Her heart lurched against her ribs. He'd only ever known a strong, warm, stable family. Until she'd come to the ranch, she hadn't given much thought to family. Certainly not on any type of personal level. In her mind, families were burdens, an unhappy blending of people forced together by a biological throw of the dice.

The Landrys were different. Or not, she acknowledged as she moistened her finger and started hunting through the pages until she found an entry for September of that year. "Shane, Dr. M," she read, drawing her lower lip between her teeth because there was no phone number, no address, not so much as a hint as to who this "Dr. M" was.

But, she realized, she had information. She had the name of the lab that had billed for the test. Maybe, just maybe, that would be enough for Chance to track down the mysterious Dr. M. She hoped so.

Tossing the date books back into the box, Taylor replaced the lid, saw movement out of the corner of her eyes and froze.

Luke Adams was standing near the entrance to the attic. "W-what are you doing?" she nearly yelped.

"Just checking on you," he stated. "Will told me to keep an eye on you. When you were gone for so long, well, I got concerned."

When her heart rate returned to normal, Taylor managed a small smile. "No need, I'm fine." She strained, attempting to lift the heavy box.

"Let me help you," he insisted, his boots scraping loudly against the floor as he rushed to her aid.

"Thanks," she breathed. She could hardly wait to get back downstairs.

Luke lifted the box with seemingly little effort, following her down the ladder.

Shane was coming along the hall, his face twisted into a dark scowl. He glared at Taylor, then looked past her, saying, "What are you doing here?"

"Uh, I was just checking on Taylor."

"*Taylor*, huh?" Shane asked, making her name sound like a curse.

"I'll be on my way," Luke said, handing the box to Taylor before hurrying off.

"Good plan," Shane commented to the ranch hand. There was a threatening glint in his eyes as he turned his gaze on Taylor. "I'm out of the house a couple of hours and you—"

"Don't finish that sentence," she warned, each syllable careful and succinct. "I understand that you're having the granddaddy of all bad days, but that doesn't give you carte blanche to take it out on me."

"What am I supposed to think?" he demanded, his voice booming.

"That I'm not the town slut?" she suggested just as forcefully.

"Really, you seemed pretty hot this morning."

Fury burned inside her. "You can be a real ass, Shane, you know that?"

Stiffening her spine, she started past him, but he reached out and grabbed her arm.

"I'm sorry, Taylor."

"Yes," she agreed, yanking herself free, "you are."

Chapter Ten

"I'm really, *really* sorry, Taylor. I didn't mean that. It was a stupid thing to say."

"You've got that right." Taylor tossed the words angrily over her shoulder. She struggled under the weight of the box, but she damn sure wasn't going to ask him for help. She would have enjoyed telling him to go away. Or at the very least, giving him a little nudge to send him head over teakettle down the steps.

He was taller, faster and very determined as he stepped around her to block the head of the stairs.

"Give it to me," he insisted, putting his hands under the box. Seeing her sag from the weight, he asked, "What do you have in there, rocks?"

"No, those would be in your head."

"I am sorry, Taylor," he repeated, not the least bit strained as he took the box, carted it down the long flight of stairs, then headed toward the kitchen, Taylor behind him.

She hated that she was distracted by watching the sway of his shoulders as he moved. Soft, worn denim hugged his trim waist, narrow hips and powerful thighs.

How was it possible to be so angry and so interested all at the same time? Luckily, her sense of urgency didn't allow for her to linger on that question.

Shane put the box on the edge of the table, sliding it toward the center and lifting the lid in one smooth, easy motion.

"Does carrying this get me out of the doghouse?" he asked, turning to face her as he absently rubbed a place near the crook of his arm.

"Not very far out," Taylor muttered, relenting. It was hard to be angry at a guy when he looked so…sad. Did men go to a special, secret class to practice that expression? That pathetic, impish, "I won't do it again, golly-gosh. Promise!" face was almost impossible to resist.

"I should never have lashed out." He took her hands in his. "I'm mad at a lot of things, but not you. Never you."

She peered up at him through the shield of her lashes. "'Never' usually only lasts until the next time."

"Come here," he said, his voice hoarse, making the request seem more like a plea.

Shane folded her against him, stroking her hair as he pressed her cheek against his chest.

She breathed in his familiar scent, listened to the strong, even rhythm of his heartbeat as her hand met his strong, solid body.

"Not with me, it doesn't," he said. "I'm not like the men your mother brought around, Taylor. Don't punish me for their sins. My remark was thoughtless—an idiotic, nasty lapse, and I promise you it won't happen again."

"Sure it will."

"I won't let it." She smelled his warm, minty breath as his lips brushed against her forehead. "Believe me?"

"It doesn't matter," she sighed, placing her arms around his waist.

"Yes, it does."

"Why?"

"Because I love you."

Taylor went still, unable to breathe, barely able to speak. "Don't" she managed to say over the lump constricting her throat.

"Too late."

Stepping out of his embrace, she stared at the tips of her shoes for a second as her eyes stung from the burn of tears she would not release. "I don't want you to love me."

"I know you've got some…issues, Taylor, and I'm the prime suspect in a murder investigation, so I'm not saying my timing is the best. But, honey," he began, bracketing her shoulders and setting her at arm's length. "Being in the middle of all this craziness has made me see that with amazing clarity. I am falling in love with you. Probably have been for years."

He looked down at her with eyes filled with sincerity.

That only made her feel worse. "I can't," she said, shaking off his touch. "I promised myself that I wouldn't even consider a serious relationship until I was well established as my own person." She saw her hand shake when she lifted it to nervously shove the hair off her face. "I'm almost twenty-eight years old and I've never even had a real job. There's—"

"What do you call the last five years?" he asked, his light eyes sparkling with humor. "Sure felt like you had a real job when I was making the quarterly tax payments."

A frustrated rush of breath spilled from her gaping mouth. Didn't he get it? "I'm the housekeeper, Shane, and while it's good, honest, decent work, it's hardly the best use of my education."

"I'm starting to wonder about that education of yours."

"Meaning?"

He stepped forward and ran the pad of his finger along the hollow of her cheek. The action caused a shiver to slink the length of her spine, before her nerve endings started tingling. The result was total sensory overload. She was aware of everything: the sound of his deep, controlled breaths each time his expansive chest rose and fell; the subtle, comforting scent of soap that lingered on his skin.

Mostly, Taylor felt need flare to life in her belly, burning more brightly now that she knew what it was like to be in his arms. To feel his hands and mouth on her body.

The shiver evolved into a violent quake that hit her with considerable force.

"Obviously, there are some areas of the human psyche they didn't tell you about in class," he teased.

"R-really?"

"Yes."

When he was close, this close, Taylor's brain cells seemed to drain of everything but her awareness of him. It was a primal, purely female awareness that made every attempt to retain reason and rationality a real struggle. Shane was temptation. It was in the soft promise of his mouth and the easy smile in his eyes. Most of all, it was knowing that it would take little more than a moment of weakness on her part and she'd be caught, hooked and reeled into the potential for a wonderful life.

But not the life she'd planned.

She stepped back, confused by the traitorous way her mind and body were derailing all the hard-and-fast rules that had gotten her this far.

The fact that Shane was giving her space actually made it worse. He simply leaned against the counter, his feet crossed at the ankles and his arms crossed lazily in front of him. It would have been easier if he'd thrown a childish fit. Anything would have been simpler than the patient, relaxed vibes emanating from him.

Shane had always been an instant-gratification guy, so this new side of him was…appealing. *Damn.*

His quiet eyes roamed over her face, then he asked, "What's in the box?"

Taylor gave herself a little mental slap and brought her thoughts back to the task. "Personal stuff," she said, tempered excitement building. Ignoring the rumble of awareness in her stomach as she moved past him, Taylor went to the box and started yanking out various date books and other items, laying them on the kitchen table as Shane came up behind her and peered over her shoulder.

Ignoring the rush of feeling caused by having his big body whisper-close to hers, Taylor thumbed through the books she'd scanned earlier, finding the entry for Dr. M. "We need the receipt from your file," she explained, flicking her thumb toward the pantry. "We'll compare the medical bills paid for the platelet test and hopefully come up with the name of the doctor."

"Good work, Nancy Drew," Shane joked as he rummaged for, then found, the paper. "Missoula Medical Center," he read.

Taylor's brow furrowed as she hunted for the phone book and skimmed through the relevant section. "Not listed."

"It was twenty-five years ago," Shane reminded her, stroking his chin. "Maybe Chance knows that lab."

While Shane made the call, Taylor moved around, trying to use up some of the annoying excess energy in her system. She felt like a cat ready to pounce, only she wasn't sure which way to leap.

It had been almost ten years since she'd mapped out her life plan. Every decision had been made with one eye on that plan. No exceptions. No deviations. Not even a mild temptation to do so. Until now. That was a sobering reality. A very scary one.

Shane's mind should have been focused only on the task at hand as he left a message for his brother. But that was hard to do when sneaking sideways glances at Taylor in her soft pink sweats. Even the loosely cut fabric couldn't hide the appealing outline of her body. A body he now knew was nothing shy of absolute perfection. He swallowed the groan in his throat, forcing his focus onto the corner of an old photograph sticking out of her pocket. Something neutral. Something that didn't remind him of the incredible sensation of holding her against him.

This wasn't the time. He rubbed his eyes as he came back to the grim reality of his situation. "The DNA has to be wrong," he muttered as he turned a chair around and straddled it.

"Or altered," Taylor suggested. "What if…" Her voice grew more animated. "What if whatever the blood work stuff you had done as a child somehow did something to your blood to skew the DNA test?"

Shane felt a twinge of optimism. "Can that happen?"

She nodded. "I read an article about a guy who had something—leukemia, I think—and because of a bone marrow transplant, his DNA was different than the other people in his family."

Shane noted the enthusiasm in Taylor's big green eyes and wanted to find it infectious. "But I don't remember any treatments. A few shots, I think. Would that be enough to screw up DNA testing?"

"We should find out," she said. "Let's go see Chance."

"Let's wait for him to call back," Shane suggested. "Even though, according to Detective Rollins, I'm the prime suspect, I've still got a ranch to run."

"What if…" Taylor paused and placed her hand on his shoulder, giving a reassuring little squeeze.

The simple, innocent gesture inspired a litany of desires in him—none of them simple and certainly not innocent. But he couldn't push. Not yet.

"What if I talk to Chance? I need to go into town, anyway."

He felt that stab of fear in his gut and it brought him back to reality. He glanced over at her, locking his eyes on hers. "Are you forgetting the calls? The shot? The note and the knife? Not going to happen, Taylor. You're staying put here on the ranch until I can make arrangements to get you away from—"

"Are you nuts? I can't leave you."

"Why is that?"

She blinked rapidly. "B-because!" she declared. "You need help, Shane. The state police think you killed your parents. I don't want you to end up like Clayton, lingering for years in some cell for a crime you didn't commit. Besides, the caller said I had to stay, and because…"

"Because?" he pressed, seeing a possible hint of the truth in those pretty eyes of hers.

She looked away. A very telling move, in his opinion. "We're friends, Shane. I'm a smart woman who just might have a skill or something that can help you. You're hardly in a position to turn down help right now."

"I have my brothers."

"What?" she demanded, jerking her face back up and glaring at him with glistening eyes that were little more than narrowed slits. "You have to be a Landry to have something to offer?"

"They love me. What's your excuse?"

"I care about you, Shane."

It took every drop of his self-control to keep from reaching out for her, taking her into his arms and proving just how inane her remark was. He was ninety-nine percent positive that she wouldn't be offering to risk her personal safety if she didn't care more than she let on. And she sure as hell wouldn't have made love to him if she wasn't just a little bit *in* love with him.

Five years, he thought, shaking his head at the perverse irony. Five years to get them to this point, and now he was a murder suspect. The gods definitely weren't smiling down on him.

"Think about it, Shane. I can't be in any real danger. As you just pointed out, I'm not a Landry. The note, the shot, the phone calls, they were all really about you. I was just the messenger."

"I don't want to see the messenger killed," he said, standing and reaching up to capture a lock of her hair between his thumb and forefinger. He let the silken strands slip through his grasp. "I'm not willing to take any chances. I've already told Seth that I want you on a plane out of Montana tomorrow."

Taylor felt her mouth drop. "Excuse me?"

"It isn't safe here for you. You've always said you wanted to visit Hawaii, so I'm sending you to—"

"I hope you bought refundable tickets," Taylor interrupted. "Aside from the fact that there's no logical reason why I would be the target of anyone, there's school. I can't just blow off my last classes and my final exams. Not after all this time."

Annoyingly, Shane shook his dark head from side to side as she spoke. "Wrong," he said with absolute finality. "I've made the arrangements, so I suggest you pack."

"I suggest you rot." She turned on her heel and started for her room.

Shane left wearing his hat, a light jacket and a slightly bemused smile that had her blood on high boil.

She was not going to be shipped off to some tropical resort like an errant child inconveniencing the family. Taylor went to her room, changed into jeans and a coral sweater, slipped on some shoes and grabbed her purse. After stuffing the faded photograph and the spotty medical information into her bag, she headed to the front door.

She got one foot outside before she was stopped by the imposing figure standing guard.

"Should have known," she muttered as she offered Will a saccharine smile. "I'm going to the store."

"Shane says you aren't."

She sidestepped the old coot. "Well, Shane is wrong."

Will's craggy fingers closed on her upper

arm. Taylor looked at his offending hand, then slowly and pointedly dragged her gaze up to meet the faded eyes of the foreman. "Are you planning on physically restraining me?"

Will looked perplexed. And annoyed. But Taylor didn't care. They stood locked in silent battle for about a minute until his hand finally dropped to his side.

"Thank you." She rooted in her purse for her keys as she started down the steps.

Will was right on her heels.

"What?" she snapped without looking at him.

"I'll come with you."

She was glad Will couldn't see the way her eyes rolled. "Suit yourself."

The trip into Jasper was long and painfully silent. She cracked the window, letting fresh air in to dilute the leathery, earthy smell of Will's lanky presence.

As it was everywhere in Montana, going to town wasn't a quick trip. Other than the dark blue truck that was little more than a blip in her rearview mirror, they were, as usual, alone on the road. She followed a forty mile ribbon of two-lane black highway that led east to the small, quaint town founded by the first Landry settlers.

Taylor liked Jasper. A beautifully manicured park lay at the center of town. At this time of year, the trees had just started to bud and bloom, adding a bright sea of chartreuse to replace the stark, barren landscape of a Montana winter.

The grass was waking from its dormant stage and the shrubs that lined Main Street were filling in nicely. Through the open window, the scent of ribs smoking behind the Cowboy Café wafted in, reminding Taylor that she hadn't eaten. Time for that after she'd spoken to Chance and dropped by Webb's Market for a little chat with Doris.

Chance Landry was the general practitioner in Jasper. His office was an old Victorian set slightly back from the road in order to accommodate a small parking lot.

It wasn't until Taylor slipped her car into a spot that Will spoke. "You sick?"

"No." She could be monosyllabic, too. She glanced at the clock on the dashboard, then added, "After I speak to Chance, I've got to get some things at the store."

"Okay."

Taylor expelled a breath. "I don't need a babysitter."

"Just watching out for you."

She thought about arguing, but knew it would prove futile. "Whatever," she said, cutting the engine, reaching for the door handle and grabbing up her purse.

Chance's nurse and receptionist, Mrs. Halloway, greeted her with a warm smile. Normally, she was perfectly coiffed, but today she looked quite harried. "Hi, Taylor, Will."

The foreman responded with a two-fingered tap to the brim of his hat. Taylor said hello, then asked, "Busy day?"

She nodded, sighing heavily. "Spring allergies. I think the whole county has been through here in the last week."

"Does Chance have a few minutes to see me?"

Mrs. Halloway nodded. "He just tried to return Shane's call. He's upstairs with Val and the baby. Want me to let him know you're coming up?"

"Please. Thanks."

"I'll wait," Will grunted, plopping into a chair and folding his arms over his chest.

Taylor shrugged, then went out the office door and walked along the gravel path leading to the staircase on the side of the building. She saw a flash of something blue out of the corner of her eye.

Heart pounding, she whipped around, feeling instantly foolish when she realized it was nothing more than a truck turning down the side street.

Mentally berating herself for being so jittery, and blaming Shane's paranoia for the effect, she took the steps two at a time, then gently rapped on the door.

Chance greeted her with the trademark Landry smile. Like all the brothers, he was tall, dark and handsome, and fairly oozed charm. In addition, he had a silly, new-father grin that probably made him more attractive.

Leaning forward, he kissed Taylor's cheek. "How are you?"

She followed him inside, astounded at the changes in the place. Thanks, no doubt, to Val, the apartment looked great.

"I haven't been here since the purging of the doilies," Taylor joked, breathing in the baby powder smell.

"I definitely don't miss the doilies and crushed velvet furniture," Chance agreed, showing her into what had once been a formal sitting room dominated by the burgundy florals that had been a favorite of the original owners. Chance had purchased the practice lock, stock and barrel from Jasper's first medical doctor, prim decor and all. But now, as she followed him through the maze of primitive prints and casual, functional furnishings, the place seemed more suited to Chance and his wife. Val was part Native American, so interspersed with high-end baby gear and toys was some really interesting and colorful folk art.

"Val should be out in a minute," he said, reaching down to scoop up a small stuffed seal from a cushion. "She's trying to get Chloe down for a nap."

As she sat, Taylor pulled the papers out of her purse. "I'm sorry to bother you, but we're trying to figure out what this means."

She filled Chance in on the blood tests and Shane's recollections of the trips to the mysterious doctor.

"Shane was ten?" Chance asked, the skin between his dark eyes wrinkling as he mulled over the thought.

"Yeah," Taylor answered. "I'm thinking it has something to do with the hinky DNA tests."

"Like what?" Chance asked.

"That's why I'm here," she explained, shifting in her chair. "Why would someone need platelet tests?"

Chance stroked his cleanly shaved chin. "Specific disorders. Suspicion of some sort of virus or disease. Hell, Taylor, there are literally thousands of things in the blood. Any of them might be of medical or clinical interest."

"Specific disorders? Inherited things?" she asked.

The gravity of the implication behind her question hung in the air between them. Taylor could almost see Chance's mind racing through all the diagnostic possibilities. To some extent, she was doing the same thing, though she was limited to general information.

"What kinds of blood things are inherited?" she asked.

Chance shook his head. "Can't be," he mumbled. "I'd know if Shane had some sort of disease, Taylor. I'm his doctor, but more importantly, I'm his brother. Believe me, if Shane had some sort of hereditary disease, there would have been some symptoms. Besides, there are seven of us. If there was some sort of family disease or condition, statistically, more than just one brother would exhibit symptoms."

"Unless he's not…" Taylor didn't want to say it aloud. Not because biology could have made him any more or less a Landry, but because it was the one thing the authorities didn't really have. Motive.

Chance's mouth pulled into a tight, grim line.

"That would explain it," he said, moving into the family room and flipping open a laptop.

Following him, Taylor was mildly distracted seeing his fingers fly across the keyboard. In the not-so-recent past, someone had tampered with Chance's patient records via the computer. Back then, Chance was barely able to boot a machine, and now, no doubt again thanks to his wife, he was as adept as an old pro. Val's computer savvy allowed her to help Chance when he really, really needed it.

Taylor felt a stab of guilt. Her attempts at assistance hadn't been quite so effective. So far, the only thing she'd discovered was a pretty decent reason why Shane might have murdered his own parents.

Chapter Eleven

Taylor's brain was pretty fried after Chance's crash course in blood disorders. When he'd promised to run tests as soon as Clayton had samples from the police lab, they switched to the issue of "Dr. M" and the Missoula Medical Center.

"I vaguely remember the place," Chance said. "It went out of business about five years ago. I'll call around and see if I can find anyone who knows where their old records are stored."

She stood and headed for the door. "Shane did not kill your parents."

Chance placed his hand on her shoulder, giving a little squeeze as she looked up into his eyes. "*Our* parents," he corrected. "No matter what, the blood tests don't matter, Taylor. Shane has to know that."

She let out a long breath. "I hope so."

"I'll walk you downstairs."

"You don't have—"

"Better safe than sorry," he insisted, placing his hand at the small of her back. "I thought Shane was putting you on a plane out of town."

Taylor shifted so she could rummage around in her purse as she walked down the steps. Will was planted at the bottom, his eyes shrouded by the brim of his hat. "I'm not running away," she said, making sure she spoke loudly enough for Will to hear as well. "Shane isn't a killer."

"That's a given. But the calls?"

She shrugged. "Aren't about me," she insisted. "Whoever is making them is desperate and doesn't know the situation. If whoever it is really wanted to motivate Shane, they'd go after one of you. Someone truly close to him and not an…employee."

"You aren't just an employee, Taylor. You've got to know how Shane feels—"

"I almost forgot—do you know these people?" she asked, taking the old photograph out of her pocket and cutting off the conversation before he could continue.

At the base of the stairs, Chance took the faded picture and studied it for several minutes. He pointed to his parents, to Doris, then to Will. "I remember this guy," he said, tapping the image of the man seated next to Will. "Not his name, just him. How about it, Will?" Chance asked. "Do you remember his name?"

Taylor watched as he passed over the photograph. After a long pause, Will shook his head, shrugged and simply mumbled, "Was a long time ago."

Snatching the picture away from the unhelpful foreman, Taylor retrieved her keys, said another goodbye to Chance and impatiently waited for Will to shadow her to the car.

She was feeling pretty useless in the grand scheme of things, and having the silent foreman in her space wasn't helping. Steering into the gravel lot behind the small store, she parked, got out and walked briskly inside.

The store was deserted, save for Doris, who was seated on a stool behind the three-foot-long counter, thumbing through a tabloid. "'Lo," Doris murmured disinterestedly.

Glancing over her shoulder, Taylor watched Will lingering by the front door. Just as well.

Doris wasn't what you'd call a happy person. Taylor frequented the market at least twice a week, more often when Sam, Callie and the kids had been living at the ranch, and she'd never been able to engage the woman in conversation.

Now, however, she wanted information from Doris, but wasn't quite sure how to approach her. Stalling as she formulated a plan, Taylor grabbed a plastic basket and looped it over her arm as she strolled down the first aisle.

The market was little more than a glorified convenience store, carrying milk, bread, eggs and enough dry goods to save locals from having to drive the extra forty miles to the closest grocery. Originally, the building had been a quaint mercantile, the center of commerce in Jasper's infancy. The plank floors were smooth and worn after a century of foot traffic. The walls had at least a dozen coats of paint, and wires hung like garlands, connecting all the twenty-first century technology not foreseen by the original builder.

Taylor glanced up at the security camera, which buzzed as it methodically swayed in an arc around the room. Absently, she tossed into the basket some coffee she didn't need and some paper towels she did. Slowly, she was summoning the nerve to approach Doris.

The salesclerk was a harsh looking woman, with every year of her life etched into the lines on her face. Thanks to the local weekly paper, Taylor knew Doris had worked at Webb's since graduating from high school. Maybe that was why she was so unhappy.

"Hi," Taylor said breathily, slightly intimidated by the sour expression on the other woman's face.

Doris grabbed for the items in the basket, glaring as she waved a glowing red wand over the bar codes. "That be all?"

"No," Taylor hedged, easing the photograph out of her purse. She slid it across the counter, keeping her forefinger on the curled edge. "Do you know these people?"

Doris shrugged. "That's me. Where'd it come from?"

"I found it at the Lucky 7 and I'm trying to identify the people in the picture."

Finally, Doris lifted her sullen brown eyes. "Why?"

Because I have to do something to help Shane? Because I'm— Not going there! "I'm just trying to organize things in light of the... *discovery.*"

"Those Landry boys can't even sort their own pictures?" the woman snorted.

"I'm just trying to help."

Doris rolled her eyes as she tapped a chipped, overly long nail on the photograph. "They don't need help, sweetie. They have everything. And I mean everything. Not real good about sharing, either. Least not after Queen Priscilla took over."

It was the first time Taylor had ever heard

anyone speak ill of Mrs. Landry. "She wasn't nice?"

Doris made a grunting sound. "She was a bitch." She paused and pulled a pack of cigarettes out from under the counter and lit one, drawing deeply before blowing a stream of blue smoke from her lips. The smoke curled up, partially obscuring the No Smoking sign taped to the wall just behind her head. "She swooped into town and sank her hooks into Caleb."

"Really?" Taylor heard nearly fifty years of bitterness in the woman's tone.

"Before she came along, Caleb and me had a thing. Can't believe he's dead. But I'll bet she had something to do with it."

"She's dead, too," Taylor reminded the woman, "so how could that be possible?"

Doris flicked ashes into a foam cup; there was a quick sizzle as hot ash fell into stale coffee. She reached up and patted her stiff, sprayed coif. "Don't you see it?" she demanded, poking at the photograph more fervently. "She was what we used to call a tease. Why, she'd flit around the Hunt Club parties like she was the belle of the ball. Looking for trouble if you ask me."

"Actually, I was asking you about the people in the picture. Do you know their names?"

Doris lifted her slightly hunched shoulders and sighed as she grabbed up the photo. "That's me and Will." She smiled briefly. "I spent an entire week's pay on that outfit. Drove all the way to Missoula to get me that store-bought dress." She took another drag of the cigarette. "In those days, we mostly made our own clothes. All of us but Priscilla, of course," Doris added with a sneer. "Leona and I went all-out that weekend."

"Leona?" Taylor prompted.

"This one," Doris said, pointing to one of the other women in the picture. "Leona Drake. She was a lot of fun, that Leona."

"Do you know where she is now?"

"Dead," Doris replied flatly. "She passed away from the female cancer five or ten years after this picture was taken. Left her useless husband and that cute little baby all alone."

Taylor was happy to let the clerk ramble on. Maybe Doris's reflections would yield something more than the name of a dead woman.

Doris signed heavily, tossing the half-smoked cigarette into the cup. "Jack was a fine-looking man in those days," she mused.

"Jack?" Taylor prompted.

"This one." Doris pointed again. "He sure went downhill in a hurry. Started drinking after he got fired."

"Fired from where?"

"Where else? The Lucky 7."

"Why'd he get fired?" Taylor asked.

"Caleb claimed he was stealing. Will backed him up. After that, no one else would hire him, so Jack just started drinking. Leona stuck it out, though. She must'a really loved him 'cause she took a job in the school cafeteria and worked them long hours even after the doctor told her about the cancer. Died with her hairnet on."

"Do you think—"

Doris raised her hand, cutting off Taylor's question in midsentence. "Take your things and go. If those Landry boys want any more information, they can pay me an hourly wage for it. You tell them I said so."

"But—"

"Go on now," Doris said, shooing her toward the door. "I've got things to do."

The woman grabbed up the tabloid and went back to reading it. Grudgingly, Taylor gathered the photograph and her grocery bag and headed for the door. At least she had something. Names. Jack and Leona Adams. If Jack was still sober, maybe he could identify the younger couple in the picture. Someone must know who they were.

Of course, it would be easier if the photograph wasn't so faded and the images were clearer. The man's face seemed familiar, but Taylor couldn't place it.

She stepped outside and found Will leaning against the edge of the building. Taylor's mind raced through possibilities. "Jack and Leona," she said. "Ring any bells?"

He just shrugged. "Yeah."

Gosh, that was helpful. She glanced across the street and had a thought. Pressing the grocery bag in Will's general direction, she mumbled something about being right back. After checking the two-lane street for traffic, Taylor jogged across to the Jasper Family Counseling Center.

A bell chimed as she opened the tinted-glass doors and went in. The small office was divided into three rooms. The reception area had a half-dozen mismatched chairs donated by various people. It smelled faintly of cherry deodorizer and was decorated with an array of framed posters and childish drawings.

Taylor smiled at the young woman behind the desk. "Hi, is Mrs. Grayson here?"

"In her office," the intern answered. "She's on the phone with someone. Can you wait a few minutes?"

Taylor nodded and thanked the fresh-faced

student. Since she was working for college credit and no pay, Taylor went out of her way to be nice to her at all times. The counseling center was far from financially stable. It was dependent on volunteers and interns to be able to offer even the most basic of services.

Grabbing up a year-old magazine, Taylor sat and tried to focus on the articles, but she wasn't terribly successful. Hopefully, Mrs. Grayson, retired social worker and lifelong Jasper resident, might be able to put names to the faces. Taylor adored the older woman, had since their first meeting. Though close to eighty, Mrs. Grayson was as sharp as a tack and full of energy. She was also a great counselor. Many of their clients remembered her from her days as a county employee. For decades, Mrs. Grayson had been the only social worker in Jasper.

The few minutes turned into ten and Taylor's nerves were beginning to fray. She wanted to identify all the people in the picture. At least then she'd feel as if she was contributing to Shane's potential defense.

Tapping her toe against the edge of the rug, she tossed aside the dated magazine and glanced outside, waiting for a dark pickup to pass before checking to see if Will was still standing guard. She didn't see him through the tinted, one-way glass, but suspected he was lurking nearby. Will was amazingly loyal, so she knew he wouldn't shirk his responsibility to Shane.

Leaning back, Taylor heard Shane's voice echo in her head: "I love you."

A knot formed in her belly. It wasn't the right time for that. Maybe, just maybe, he'd wait. Probably not. He preferred instant gratification, and she had no idea how long it might take for her to establish herself in…what? Private practice? No bites on her résumé thus far. Teaching? Nothing there either. She drummed her nails on the arms of the chair. Forget career aspirations. What if Shane got arrested? Worse yet, what if he was convicted? Was that even possible? Could lightning strike the family twice?

Clayton had spent more than four years in prison for a crime he didn't commit. Was it possible that a second Landry brother could suffer the same fate?

She rubbed her face, then pressed her fingers into her temples. *I can't think like that. I have to stay positive and focused and…* Her heart squeezed inside her chest. How had everything gotten so complicated? *Because they found the bodies?*

No, it wasn't just that.

Because I slept with him?

No, it wasn't just that.

Because I'm in love with him?

Taylor shook her head, refusing to entertain thoughts that would completely derail her life plan. Like every other time she'd faced an obstacle, she had to fix this and move forward. That was the only way to make sure she didn't fall into the family pattern.

The door to the hallway leading to twin modest offices opened. Mrs. Grayson smiled. She leaned heavily on a cane. "This is a surprise."

"I need some help," Taylor said, standing and digging through her purse at the same time. "I found a photograph and I'm trying to identify the people."

"Nice to see you, too," her friend stated, placing her free hand at her ample waist. "Come on inside and we'll catch up. You haven't been here for two weeks."

"Sorry," Taylor muttered. "I guess I'm just flustered by everything that's been going on."

Mrs. Grayson looped her arm through Taylor's, ushering her down the narrow hall toward her practically barren office. "Are you sure that's all it is?"

Taylor sat down in a dated armchair they'd found at a local yard sale a year earlier. She held out the picture when the older woman had settled into her chair and balanced her cane against the arm. "Do you recognize this man or this woman?" She pointed.

Mrs. Grayson lifted the glasses dangling from a chain of brightly colored beads around her neck. "Well, well, this takes me back."

Taylor scooted forward and named the people she'd already identified. "The man looks familiar, but I can't place him."

"He does," Mrs. Grayson agreed. "Because it's a very young Brian Hollister."

"Senator Brian Hollister?' Taylor asked.

Mrs. Grayson nodded, the tight bun at the crown of her head bobbing. Lowering her glasses, she turned her inquisitive gaze on Taylor. "He couldn't have been twenty in this picture. Why does it matter?"

Taylor filled the woman in on what had been happening. As expected, the older woman's well-practiced expression didn't reveal anything she might be thinking. "I see. So, you're now on a mission to save the man you don't love?"

Taylor winced. "I didn't say that. I—I care about Shane."

"I think it's more than that," she countered.

"Not now," Taylor insisted, momentarily distracted by the sounds of approaching sirens outside. "Even if I did feel *something,* the timing couldn't be worse."

Mrs. Grayson offered a knowing smile. "Love has a way of cropping up at the most inopportune time."

"Not to me," Taylor said, perhaps more for herself than her companion. "I'm not going to perpetuate the family pattern."

"Ever think you've already broken the cycle of bad relationships?"

"No," Taylor admitted. "I have to be a whole person."

"Ever think you are a whole person already?"

Taylor reclaimed the photograph. "Has anyone ever told you you ask too many questions?"

"Occupational hazard," Mrs. Grayson said with a pronounced sigh. "You're a twenty-seven-year-old woman, Taylor, who, in my opinion, should be smart enough to see that you long ago stopped needing your unfortunate childhood as motivation."

"No, I haven't," Taylor insisted, gathering up her purse.

"Really? Then why are you so scared?"

"Because some lunatic has threatened us."

"Us?"

Taylor regarded her friend for a moment. "Don't analyze my every word."

"Can't help it. But I'll stop if you'll stop making Shane pay for the wrongs of the likes of Duane Treadwell."

"I'm not. I've got to—"

"Come quick!" the intern yelled as she rushed in.

"What happened?" Taylor asked.

"It's Doris."

Taylor's blood stilled in her veins. "Webb's Market Doris?"

The intern nodded. "There's police cars, and somebody said she's dead. Someone shot her."

Chapter Twelve

A gathering crowd formed a semicircle around the half-block radius cordoned off in front of the market. The acrid smell of burning rubber filled Shane's nostrils after he brought the SUV to a screeching halt in the center of Main Street and flung open his door.

Information relayed to the ranch was sketchy. He knew only that there had been a shooting in town.

Taylor.

Shielding his eyes with his hands, he stood on the truck's running board and scanned the crowd. His heart stopped when he didn't see her among the assembled faces. He knew he'd never be able to forgive himself if so much as a single hair on her head was out of place.

Jumping down, he strode purposefully through the crowd, lifting the yellow tape and ducking beneath it as he kept searching for a glimpse of her. Stepping sideways between the ambulance and a fire truck, he approached a small group of deputies and paramedics.

"Where's Seth?" he demanded.

"Inside," one of them answered.

A uniformed man he recognized as a rookie deputy looked as if he might block Shane's path. One pointed glare was all it took for the guy to step aside.

Just inside the doorway, a white sheet with the name of the local mortuary stenciled on the hem covered the still outline of a body. As he came closer, Shane found it impossible to take a breath. His heart literally squeezed so hard he was sure it would explode at any second. A tight, dry sensation strangled him as he took in the scene.

He was about a foot away when her name erupted from his lips in an anguished cry.

The activity in the room turned into a dull buzz in his ears. His gaze remained fixed on the blood, the body, and he had the very real feeling that someone had reached into his chest and ripped his heart out.

"Shane?"

It took a moment for the voice to penetrate his shock-numbed brain. Whipping his head around, he felt relief wash over him in crashing waves when he saw Taylor step out from one of the aisles.

He practically scooped her off the ground, holding her so tightly he could feel the breath rush from her small frame. He planted kiss after kiss on her hair, her forehead, pretty much any part of her he could reach before putting her down and sliding his palms up to cup her face.

He saw fear, torment and guilt in her eyes, but it didn't matter. She was safe. She was... "What the hell happened?"

Taylor blinked at the harshness of his tone. "There was a robbery. Doris was shot."

After placing one last kiss on her forehead, Shane cradled her against him and surveyed the scene over her head. Seth was huddled with a guy from the medical examiner's office. Chance was off in another corner, talking to a paramedic who was making notes on a clipboard. Will was back by the small dairy case, a quiet observer with his hat in his hand.

"Were you here? Are you hurt?" Shane set her at arm's length.

Taylor shook her head. "No, no. I was across the street with Mrs. Grayson. We ran over here when the emergency vehicles started to arrive."

"Thank God," he murmured, hugging her to him again. "When I heard the news I was so afraid it was you. I've never been so scared in my life. The whole way into town I was sure something terrible had happened to you."

"It didn't," she insisted, settling her cheek against his chest. "But it was a close call. I was in here talking to Doris not fifteen minutes before the shooting. Luckily, though, Will was outside the center waiting for me. So I think I heard him tell Seth he could give a description of the robber."

"So, it was really a robbery?" Shane asked.

"I know. I don't think it was either," Taylor said, apparently reading his thoughts. "If Will hadn't been here to witness the getaway, I'd be thinking the same thing. Jasper doesn't have much in the way of crime so the coincidence is kind of...*creepy*."

"That's one way of putting it," Shane agreed. He brushed his lips on her forehead. Leaning back, he gently squeezed her forearms and smiled down at her in relief. "Will you be okay if I go talk to Seth and Will for a minute?"

She pointed toward the door. "I'm going back across the street. I've already given my statement, and frankly, I don't like being in here with poor Doris's body. Do you mind?"

He shook his head. "Shouldn't be a problem. The street is crawling with cops and firemen and most of the town. Just to be on the safe side, I'll walk you over there, then I'll come back in a bit to take you home to the ranch."

Once he had Taylor safely secured behind the locked door of the Family Counseling Center, he jogged back to join his brothers, just as Doris's corpse was being wheeled out to the waiting ambulance. Several shocked gasps sounded in the crowd as the gurney was lifted and the doors slammed shut.

Will was waiting for him at the doorway to the market. "Glad you were with her," Shane said, extending his hand. "Taylor said you saw the shooter?"

The foreman nodded. "Tall, young, mid-twenties, thirty on the outside. Ran out of the market and hauled ass around the corner. Then a blue pickup truck squealed out of here heading north."

"Did you hear a shot?"

"Not so I could swear," Will said, almost apologetically. Shane watched as his longtime friend broke eye contact to stare off into space. "I wish I could have helped."

"I know you do," Shane said, patting the older man on the shoulder in hopes it might assuage some of the guilt he read in Will's expression. "Too bad about Doris, but I'm glad Taylor is safe. Thank you for that."

Will shifted from foot to foot awkwardly, which was very in keeping with the man's personality. Will kept everything close to the vest, so Shane was sure it was uncomfortable for a stoic guy like him to accept gratitude, compliments or any other remotely overt emotional response.

"Want me to drive her car back to the ranch?" Will offered.

"Good idea. Mind getting the keys yourself? I want to have a word with Seth."

"Consider it done. See you back at the spread."

Shane breathed his first genuine sigh of relief as he went in search of Seth. His heartbeat had finally calmed and the knotted muscles in his shoulders were slowly relaxing. Rolling his head to dispatch the last bit of tension, he again bypassed the deputies and stepped inside the somber building.

"…Dust every inch of this place," Seth was telling the crime scene tech. "And copy the tapes from the security cameras and send them to my office."

"Will do, Sheriff Landry."

Seth turned, his expression hard. "This stinks," he muttered as he grabbed Shane's arm and led him away from the others, waving for Chance to join them.

"It's a shame," Shane agreed. "Doris has been a fixture around town."

"That, too," Seth said, his voice quiet as he huddled together with his brothers. "I mean, it's bad she's dead, but this whole thing doesn't feel right."

"How so?" Chance asked.

Shane watched as Seth glanced down at his notepad. "The money from the lockbox under the counter is gone but the register wasn't touched."

"Meaning that most criminals are, as they say, all hat and no cattle. That's hardly newsworthy," Chance offered.

"Meaning," Shane suggested, "the perpetrator knew the place. Knew Doris kept the money from lottery sales in the box under the counter. Knew she kept little more than the float in the cash register."

Seth agreed. "Yeah, except they pulled the numbers night before last. If you were going to rob this place, wouldn't you do it the day after a ton of tickets had been sold? Increase your take?"

"Sure, right. So why wait the extra day when the lottery money would already be in the bank, and then leave the register untouched?" Chance asked.

"It could be a stupid criminal moment, or

it could be something else," Shane agreed. "Was Taylor the last person in here before the robbery?"

Seth nodded. "According to Will, no one came in after she left except a tall white male in jeans and a beige Stetson who we have to assume is the perp."

"That describes roughly half the population of Montana." Glancing over his shoulder, Shane asked, "What about the cameras?"

"Look more closely," Seth answered.

When he did, Shane noticed that there was a film of something on the lens. Moving to within a few feet of where the camera was mounted in the corner of the room, he saw a puddle on the floor. "What's this?"

"Shaving cream," Seth muttered. "I haven't seen the tape, but I'm betting whoever it was covered it with foam."

"Smart," Shane acknowledged.

Seth blew out a frustrated breath. "I'm crossing my fingers that the camera got a look at him before he screwed with the lens."

"If the guy was smart enough to disable the camera, why not do a better job of the robbery?" Shane asked of no one in particular.

"That's another thing," Seth said. "Told you it feels wrong."

Shane met his brother's perplexed expression. "You're thinking the robbery was just to cover up killing Doris?"

"Too soon to tell, but I'm not buying the idea that my town is suddenly the crime capital of the county. I mean, what are the odds of someone taking a shot at Taylor, and then a few days later, a store clerk gets killed minutes after talking to her?"

Shane felt the blood in his veins turn icy. "You think there's a connection?"

"I do."

"I AGREE," Taylor said, shivering when she admitted as much to Shane a few minutes into their drive back to the ranch. She recounted her conversation with Doris, glossing over the very unflattering picture the bitter clerk had painted of Priscilla Landry. "I think Doris was killed to send a message."

"Which is?" Shane prompted.

Taylor drew her bottom lip between her teeth as she continued racking her brain for some connection that made sense. "She knew the history, Shane. I think she knew something else, too."

"Why?"

"Because she hinted that she'd be willing to sell it to you."

"What?"

"At the time, I thought she was just being… unpleasant. But she pretty much said that if the Landrys wanted information from her, they'd have to pay. It never occurred to me that she was serious."

Taylor turned, stealing a peek at his handsome profile. Shane's long hair was pulled back into a loose ponytail, secured with a soft leather cord. Tension was etched into deep lines at the edge of his mouth. Sighing heavily, she tugged at the shoulder belt and tucked one leg under her as she tried to think of some scenario that might logically explain the murder of a surly store clerk.

She was distracted when Shane reached over to rest his hand on her knee. Distracted didn't exactly cover it. His fingers felt like Tazers, sending pulses of electricity through her bloodstream.

Taylor hated herself for thinking vivid, carnal thoughts so soon after Doris's unfortunate demise. She justified it by reminding herself that it wasn't as if she and Doris had been friends. The woman didn't have any friends. Except for Leona, who was also dead.

Completely frustrated, Taylor shoved her hair off her forehead and tried to focus. Impossible. Shane was tracing maddening little circles against her thigh with his thumb. Even through her jeans, the brush of his touch ignited a small blaze in her belly.

She needed to get herself in check before they reached the ranch. If she didn't, she wouldn't trust herself not to do something foolish. Again.

"You're tensing," Shane remarked, punctuating his observation with a gentle squeeze. "What's wrong?"

Taylor turned and glanced at the passing scenery. She didn't want to have this conversation. She wasn't ready to have it. Besides, what could she say? *Shane, I want you so badly my whole body is coiled with need, but*—and it was a big but—*I'm scared I won't be able to walk away. And if I don't walk away, if I don't become my own person, I'll hate myself. And you.*

"It's been a tough morning," she remarked, hearing the overwhelming sadness in her own voice.

Shane must have heard it, too, because he said, "There's something else bothering you, Taylor. What is it?"

"Nothing," she insisted. Classic conflict-avoidance, she decided as they turned up the long driveway leading to the main house. "I'm just drained, I guess."

"You should lie down when we get home."

"Maybe," she agreed, in little more than a murmur.

It was a really beautiful late afternoon, which seemed almost disrespectful in light of recent events. Still, she couldn't help but appreciate the striking scenery. The Lucky 7 Ranch was a massive spread rimmed by the Rockies. Snow-capped mountains bracketed three sides of the ranch house built by Shane's grandfather. Along with the main house, there were several outbuildings—three barns, a bunkhouse, a smokehouse and some storage sheds.

Sam, the eldest of the Landry brothers, had just finished construction of a home for his rapidly growing family on the eastern edge of the property. Taylor missed them, especially the children. There was something homey about the smell of baby powder and the shriek of little children playing. Even though their new place was technically on the ranch, it was at least a fifteen minute drive from the main house.

Shane parked in the horseshoe-shaped driveway in front of the massive home. They climbed the front steps and were approaching the large mahogany doors when she felt Shane's hand at the small of her back.

His splayed fingers inspired a little shiver to dance along her spine. She closed her eyes briefly, taking in the familiar, comforting scent of his cologne.

"I want you to go lie down," he said, latching the door and guiding her toward her room. "I've got to check in with Will."

"I should start dinner."

"Forget it," Shane grunted. "We'll wing it tonight."

"You don't pay me to wing it."

"Yeah, well, consider yourself on paid leave."

They reached her room. Shane. Bed. *Bad.* Taylor's whole body was on alert. High alert. The walls felt as if they would close in on her at any moment. Shane's presence shrunk the space, aided by the strong, heady desire pulling her insides into taut knots.

His hand fell away when he reached around her and tugged down the comforter. "Take a break, Taylor." He patted the soft mattress. "I'll be back in a while."

It took all of her personal strength to keep from begging him to stay with her. But she managed, feeling alone and lonely when he pulled the blanket over her and kissed her on the forehead before leaving.

Taylor's heart actually hurt. This would all be over soon. A memory she'd surely revisit for the rest of her life. She'd worked too hard, come too far to change gears now. But what if Shane was arrested? It seemed as if the cosmos were conspiring to steal what little time they had left.

What to do?

Squeezing her eyes closed, she weighed the possibilities. Was she capable of having a casual affair with him? Was it really casual? No, he cared for her. And she…what? Admitting her true feelings, acknowledging them—even to herself—was not an option. That was about the only certainty in her life just then.

SHANE WAS ON HIS THIRD cup of coffee when he heard the water from Taylor's shower cut off. He took a long swallow of the muddy sludge, hoping his brain would focus on the hot liquid searing his throat. No such luck. What burned most was his fierce need to be with her. Pictures of Taylor naked and wet, standing under the stream of the shower, slipped in and out of his mind. He groaned aloud and suffered in silence as he heard her hair dryer, then the drawers, then finally the sound of her bare feet as she came down the hallway.

Normally, he would have been impressed by her display of inner strength. By the way she always managed to soldier on, regardless of the situation. He'd seen it every time a family crisis loomed. But this wasn't normal. Not by a long shot.

Normal didn't include his fascination with the smell of floral shampoo that arrived a split second before she came into the kitchen, wearing a plain white robe that seemed anything but plain when wrapped around her incredible body.

He allowed his eyes to roam freely and happily over her upturned face. He knew he should offer some sort of greeting, but he was afraid if he opened his mouth at that moment, it would be to insist that they go back to her bedroom.

As if reading his mind, Taylor stood still, her thickly lashed hazel eyes focused on him. Her lips parted slightly, allowing each breath to ease in and out of her pretty mouth.

A moan of strong, urgent need rumbled in Shane's throat. He felt a seizure in his gut and a tightness in his groin as his gaze dropped lower, to her long, delicate throat, and then lower still, to the hint of cleavage just above the V formed by the neckline of her robe.

Banishing rational thought from his brain, Shane took the two steps necessary to reach her, wrapped his arm around her waist and dragged her against him. The feel of her body against his was like finding his own personal little slice of heaven.

He wanted to take it slowly, intended to, in fact. But intentions were a memory the minute he dipped his head to brush his lips on hers. He felt the warmth of her mouth and tasted cool mint as his tongue teased her lips apart.

Taylor flattened her hands against his chest, enjoying the strong beat of his heart beneath her touch. Reluctantly, he loosened his grip and she stepped back ever so slightly.

Her eyes roamed boldly over the vast expanse of his shoulders, drinking in the contours of his impressive upper body where his shirt was tightly pulled. She openly admired the powerful thighs straining against the soft fabric of his jeans. The mere sight caused a fluttering in the pit of her stomach.

"So…" Her voice was soft and sultry, her eyes hot. "What are we going to do about this, since our respective self-control seems to have gone right out the window? I'm thinking it would be stupid for us not to sleep together."

"I agree." His voice was shallow, his breathing uneven. "I want you. But we aren't children," he felt compelled to point out. "We can't have everything we want."

"Does that mean you want me as badly as I want you?" Taylor held her breath, waiting for his reply.

He met her gaze. "Right now, your *safety* should by my primary concern. I should be putting you on a plane and getting you out of harm's way while I figure out who killed my parents."

Her arms wound about his neck. "I hear a but in there."

"Not a but." Shane smiled. "An 'on the other hand.' I want to stay close to you. Very, very close."

"I think we could get a lot closer in the bedroom, don't you?" she asked, unable to keep from smiling. She looked up at him, enjoying the anticipation fluttering in her stomach. The clock on the wall showed six-fifteen.

"You shouldn't make these kinds of offers, Taylor. Not unless you mean them."

She rose up on tiptoe to kiss his chin. "You know me. I rarely say anything I don't mean."

"We have that in common," he commented as he brushed his lips against her forehead.

Taylor took a deep breath and went for it. "Look, Shane. I'm asking you to go to bed with me. Nothing else. I need to be clear on that."

He moved and pulled her into the circle of his arms. "I wasn't expecting this."

"Me either," she admitted easily, adding, "I haven't been able to think of much of anything but you since we…since the last time."

Feeling safe and protected in the circle of his arms, Taylor closed her eyes. It would be wonderful to forget everything—all the baggage, all the danger. Just for a few hours. No memory of the calls, the knife, Doris, none of it. Nothing but the magic of being with Shane.

His fingers danced over her back, leaving a trail of electrifying sensations. Like a spring flower, passion blossomed deep within her, filling her quickly with a frenzied desire she had felt only once before. He ignited feelings that were powerful and intense.

Then he slipped the tip of his finger inside the neckline of her robe and she couldn't think anymore. Except maybe to consider begging when he stopped.

Shane moved his hand in slow, sensual circles until it rested against her rib cage, just under the swell of her breast. He wanted—no, needed—to see her face. He wanted to see the desire in her eyes. Catching her chin between his thumb and forefinger, he tilted her head up with the intention of searching her eyes. He never made it that far.

His gaze was riveted to her lips, which were slightly parted, a glistening pale rose. He could feel her pulse rate increase through the fabric of her robe.

Lowering his head, he took another tentative taste. Her mouth was warm and pliant. So was her body, which now pressed urgently against him. His hands roamed purposefully, memorizing every nuance and curve.

He felt his own body respond with an ache, then an almost overwhelming rush of desire surged through him. Her arms slid around his waist, pulling him closer. Shane marveled at the perfect way they fit together. It was as if she had been made for him. For this.

"Taylor," he whispered against her mouth. He toyed with a lock of her hair, then slowly wound his hand through the silken mass and gave a gentle tug, forcing her head back even more. Looking down at her face, Shane decided there was no other sight on earth as beautiful and inviting as her smoky hazel eyes.

In one effortless motion, he lifted her, carried her to her bedroom and carefully lowered her onto the bed. Her light hair fanned out against the pillow.

"I think you're supposed to get on the bed with me," Taylor said in a husky voice when he remained perched at the edge of the mattress.

With one finger, Shane reached out to trace the delicate outline of her mouth. Her skin was the color of ivory, tinged with a faint, warm flush.

Sliding into place next to her, he began showering her face and neck with light kisses. While his mouth searched for that sensitive spot at the base of her throat, he felt her fingers working the buttons of his shirt.

He waited breathlessly for the feel of her hands on his body and he wasn't disappointed when anticipation gave way to reality. A moan of pleasure spilled from his mouth when she brushed away his clothing and began running her palms over the muscles of his stomach.

Capturing both of her hands in one of his, Shane gently held them above her head. The position arched her back, drawing his eyes down to the outline of her erect nipples.

"This isn't fair," she said as he slowly untied the belt of her robe.

"Believe me, Taylor, if I let you keep touching me, I'd probably last less than a minute," he assured her with a smile and a kiss.

Taylor responded by lifting her body to him. The rounded swell of one breast brushed his arm, and he began peeling away the terry cloth covering her. He was rewarded by an incredible view of her breasts spilling over the edges of a lacy bra that was sexy as sin. His eyes burned as he drank in the sight of taut peaks straining against the lace. His hand rested against her flat stomach, then began inching up the warm flesh. Finally, his fingers closed over the rounded fullness.

"Please let me touch you!" Taylor cried.

"Not yet," he whispered, releasing the front clasp on her bra. He ignored her futile struggle to free her hands, and dipped his head to kiss the raging pulse point at her throat. Her soft skin grew hot as he worked his mouth lower and lower. She gasped when his lips closed around her nipple, then called his name in a hoarse voice that caused a tremor to run the full length of his body.

Moments later, he lifted his head long enough to see her passion-filled expression and to tell her she was beautiful.

"So are you."

Whether it was the sound of her voice or the way she pressed against him, Shane neither knew nor cared. He found himself nearly un done by the level of passion communicated by the movements of her supple body.

He reached down until his fingers made contact with a wisp of silk and lace that almost constituted enough to be labeled panties. The feel of the sensuous garment against her skin very nearly pushed him over the edge. With her help, he was able to whisk the thong over her hips and legs, until she was finally next to him without a single barrier.

He sought her mouth again as he finally released his hold on her hands. He didn't know which was more potent, the feel of her naked against him or the frantic way she worked to remove his clothing. His body moved to cover hers, his tongue thrusting deeply into the warm recesses of her mouth. He ran his hand downward, skimming the side of her flesh all the way to her thigh. Then, giving in to the urgent need pulsating through him, Shane positioned himself between her legs. Every muscle in him tensed as he looked at her face, before directing his attention lower, to the point where they would join.

Taylor lifted her hips, welcoming, inviting,

as her palms grasped his flanks and tugged him toward her.

"You're incredible," he groaned against her lips.

"Thank you," she whispered back. "I want you. Now, please?"

He wasted no time responding to her request. In a single motion, he thrust deeply inside of her, knowing without question that he had found his own personal paradise.

He wanted to treat her to a slow, building climax, but with the feelings sweeping through him, it wasn't an option. He caught his breath and held it. The sheer pleasure of being inside of her sweet softness was just too powerful. She wrapped her legs around his hips as the first explosive waves surged through him. One after the other, ripples of pleasure poured from him into her. Satisfaction had never been so sweet.

With his head buried next to hers, the sweet scent of her hair filled his nostrils. Shane reluctantly relinquished possession of her body. It took several minutes before his breathing slowed to a steady, satiated pace.

Rolling onto his side next to her, he rested his head against his arm and glanced down at her. She was sheer perfection. He could have happily stayed with her in the big, soft bed until the end of time.

Sadly, the telephone rang just then, disturbing the lazy tranquility of the moment. Taylor flinched at the strident sound. "I don't want to answer that."

Shane knew how she felt. "I'd better. Could be one of my brothers with news."

"I know."

He reached for the receiver. "Hello?" Instantly alert, Taylor read the absolute shock in Shane's eyes as he listened to the caller.

Chapter Thirteen

"What?" Taylor asked Shane as he hung up the phone.

"Something from the tape."

"The killer? That's fantastic!"

Shane's face was a mask of concentration as he shook his head. He shrugged into his shirt. "If that was the case, Seth would've told me. He just said it wasn't something he could explain over the phone. Said I had to see it."

"That's a little cryptic," Taylor offered as she hid behind the partially closed closet door in order to dress. Which, if she thought about it, was silly. Shane had already seen everything.

Curiosity piqued, she was grateful to have something to focus on aside from her sudden shyness and her complete and utter lack of self-control. She'd deal with her behavior later, as soon as she thought up a plausible way to rationalize her reasons for having sex with Shane a second time.

After running her fingers through her hair, she stepped into flat shoes and joined Shane in the foyer. There really was no way to rationalize her body's immediate and primordial response to him. She absolutely tingled, and all he was doing was standing by the door, waiting for her.

Sex was supposed to have been the scratch for this itch. Surely satisfaction should last more than an hour. It wasn't emotionally healthy to want someone the way she wanted Shane. How many times had she offered such counsel to people? Explained that burning passion is usually temporary and rarely a good foundation on which to build a relationship?

What relationship? that annoying little voice in her mind shouted.

The one I'm not doing a very good job of avoiding.

"Sorry to drag you out so quickly," Shane said as he tugged her jacket off the brass coat tree by the door and handed it to her with a wink. "Believe me when I tell you I'd much rather have spent the whole night doing any number of wonderful things to your body and mind."

"Don't worry about doing things to my mind," she muttered as she walked with him toward the SUV. "I've pretty much got that area covered."

She heard Shane expel a loud breath, not that he'd done much of anything to hide the frustration fairly oozing from his pores.

"Damn it, Taylor. I can practically see that mind of yours working at full throttle. Still trying to convince yourself that there's nothing between us but excellent sex?"

"There *is* nothing more between us than excellent sex." Of course there was, but the second she put *those* thoughts out there, she'd be lost. "Which," she hastened to add, "is exactly as it should be. We're adults. Nothing wrong with us both wanting a satisfying sexual relationship. Neither of us needs to give up anyth—"

"Who's asking you to give anything up?" He was clearly annoyed. "I don't remember making any demands on you."

"You said you cared for me."

"I do. Consider the declaration, and the sentiment behind it, a gift. Not an obligation. At least it's supposed to be." When she didn't respond, Shane slanted his gaze in her direction. She was staring out of the window, her jaw set. *Stubborn woman.* He restrained himself from pulling over to the side of the road and kissing her senseless, or, he thought with an inner smile, loving the woman into submission. "Stop being obtuse and so damn single-minded about this," he told her, consciously taking the heat out of his words.

He didn't need Taylor's acceptance of his declaration to know that she just might be as crazy in love with him as he was with her. All he needed was the patience of a saint and the willpower of a monk.

It chafed to know that Taylor's position hadn't changed. Shane wondered what he'd have to do to get her to at least open up to the possibility that loving him wouldn't sound the death knell to her dreams and aspirations. Not an easy task given the reality of his situation. His timing couldn't be worse.

He turned the truck onto the highway, knowing he had to put things in the proper sequence. First, he needed to find a way out from under the dark cloud of suspicion. Hopefully, whatever Seth was onto would point him in that direction. Then he'd find some way to convince Taylor that loving him wouldn't ruin her life.

"Apparently our postcoital glow has disappeared," he said dryly. "How long are you going to give me the silent treatment?"

"I have nothing to contribute to the conversation."

He had volumes to contribute, but he bit his tongue. Time for that later. "Then feel free to open a new topic of conversation to while away the time it'll take us to get there."

Their eyes met. "Go, Grizzlies?"

Shane grinned as he brought his attention back to the road. God he loved her.

He parked in a spot adjacent to the municipal building in the heart of Jasper, and forced himself to change his focus.

Barely aware of the chill settling in the early evening air, he and Taylor climbed the steps and headed toward the door with Sheriff's Office stenciled in bold, black letters above a replica of the star his brother wore pinned to his uniform.

Taylor took his hand as they passed through the hinged, wooden half door that led past the secretary's desk. It was so distracting to feel her soft, warm fingers lace with his that Shane stammered when he greeted Lucy, the night dispatcher.

"Sheriff's expecting you," Lucy offered, continuing to file her fingernails as she spoke. "Hey, Taylor. Nice sweater."

Seth was seated on the edge of his desk. The chairs were pushed together to make room for a small cart with a television set and videotape player. He had his thumb on the remote control, rewinding and playing the grainy image from Webb's Market.

"Recognize him?" Seth asked without greeting as he continued to replay the tape.

Taylor stared at the screen, scrutinizing the partially obscured figure of a man who kept his head bowed as he approached the camera, then without looking up, raised the hand holding the can of shaving cream to obliterate the image.

A large, light-colored Stetson hid his face. The security camera tape was black-and-white, so it was impossible to identify even the basics.

"Not me," Shane said.

Taylor moved closer. "Can you play it slower?"

"Yep." Seth rewound to the moment the man entered the market. "He brought the shaving cream with him."

The poor quality image flickered as about one quarter of the man's body remained visible in the left side of the frame. Then the shaving cream, then nothing.

"Again, please?"

"See something?" Shane asked, moving his hand to her shoulder as he leaned in close.

His warm breath caressed her cheek as she

struggled to remain focused on the videotape. "What's that?" she asked, touching the tip of her finger to the screen.

Tilting her head, she waited for Seth to rewind and freeze one frame in particular. It was a close-up of the man's hand. Part of it, at least.

Squinting, Taylor stared at the hand, specifically the knuckles. "See that?" she asked, feeling a rush of excitement as she pointed to the dark spots.

"A shadow, maybe?" Shane offered.

She shook her head, exuberantly declaring, "Tattoos."

"Yes, maybe," Shane said. "But they're too blurry to make out. Is there some computer tech that can—"

"We don't need one," Taylor practically sang. "I know only one person around town who has tattooed knuckles. Luke Adams."

"I know that name," Shane said. "He works for me. He's one of the new hires."

Shane grabbed Taylor and planted a quick kiss on her open mouth. "I don't care what they say, you are not just a pretty face, Taylor Reese."

She felt herself grinning like a child as she fought the urge to leap into his arms. Instead, she turned to Seth and asked, "Can you go out to the ranch and arrest him?"

"Already on it," Seth said, reaching for the phone and his hat in one smooth motion. "Have all cars roll to the Lucky 7," he told the dispatcher.

Feeling quite impressed with herself, Taylor took one last look at the screen as she started for the door. She stopped. "Wait. Look. See the door to the dairy case?" The Landry brothers did as she instructed, moving in close to where she pointed. "Doesn't that look like a man?"

"Hard to tell," Shane hedged. "The quality is so poor."

Taylor was almost certain she saw the faint image of a man's reflection in the glass. "It looks like a man to me."

"I don't think so, Taylor," Seth said. "Will only saw one perp. Thanks to your keen observation, we have a pretty good idea who he is. You two hang back."

"Why?" Taylor asked.

"In case there's trouble. Luke Adams has an arrest record. No telling what he'll do when he's confronted."

"Seth's right, Taylor," Shane stated. "I'm going to drop you off at Chance's place. You can stay there while we go after Adams."

Her shoulders slumped. "That's not fair.

I'm the one who identified him. I should be... well, included."

Shane shot her a glance softened by his very sexy, lopsided smile. "Really? What are you planning to do if he resists arrest? Beat him into submission with inkblots?"

"I'm saving that for you," she quipped. "I could be of help, Shane."

"Really? How?"

"Well..." She paused to take a deep breath while Seth was busy checking his gun before snapping it into the holster. "I could reason with Luke. The kind of thing a hostage negotiator might do."

"I'm not planning on taking any hostages, but thanks all the same," Shane said.

Seth rounded the desk, hat and keys in hand. "You two can stay here and fight it out. I'm going after the bad guy."

Ten minutes later, Taylor found herself seated in Chance and Val's above-the-office family room. Baby Chloe was teetering on the brink of sleep as she rested against her father's shoulder. Val was in the small kitchen, brewing some tea she insisted would relax Taylor's anxiety in no time flat.

Fat chance, she thought as she fidgeted in her seat. Taylor managed a weak smile when Val handed her a steaming cup of tea that smelled faintly of cranberry. "Thanks." She took a sip to be polite and found the blend of herbal tea and fruit actually was soothing. "Should we call the ranch?" she asked.

Chance and Val smiled at each other, then looked at Taylor with a great deal of patience and compassion. Val spoke. "Honey, would you please put Chloe to bed? Just rock her for a while first."

"My pleasure." With the baby cradled in his arms, Chance disappeared down the narrow hallway, leaving the two women alone. Taylor felt her insides wind into a tight coil as the passage of time seemed to slow to an unnatural crawl.

Val patted her hand as she flopped next to her on the sofa, tucking one long leg under her body in an easy motion. "Hang in there. Seth and Shane will get to the bottom of this."

"I can't stand the waiting," Taylor sighed, raking her fingers through her hair after setting the cup on the coffee table. Sensing a change in Val's mood, Taylor asked, "What?"

"I found something," she answered, her voice low and her tone guarded.

"What kind of something?"

Jumping up, Val retrieved her laptop and brought it over to the sofa. "Chance and I have been researching DNA and the platelet test Shane had as a child. We've also been having the blood samples taken by the state police analyzed."

"And?" Taylor asked, feeling her heart rate increase from the anticipation.

"Von Willebrand disease."

Taylor said the words in her mind over and over. "Sound's bad."

Val shook her head vehemently, again patting Taylor's knee. "No, really. I mean, it can be, but it can also be a mild condition that goes undiagnosed until some catastrophic event."

"Shane has this...*illness?*" Her mouth was so dry it was difficult to get the question out. All sorts of questions ran through her mind. "How bad is it? Is he going to die? How did he get it?"

"Slow down." Val cautioned, her expression calm and patient. "I'll do my best to explain it to you. Whatever I can't answer, I'm sure Chance can. Know anything about blood disorders?"

"Close to nothing," Taylor admitted. "I think I read a story in a magazine about a woman who was struggling with a rare form of leukemia. Is that what this is? A form of cancer? Is that why the blood tests from the crime scene incriminated Shane?"

"No," Val insisted with some amount of force. "Von Willebrand's is a distant cousin to hemophilia. Simply speaking, a person with this condition might experience symptoms like bleeding from the gums, slow healing and frequent bruising."

"Bruising?" Taylor repeated, her mind's eye flashing the countless times she'd seen deep purplish bruises on some part of Shane's body. She'd never given them a second thought, which now made her feel intense guilt. "Val, I've—"

"We all have," Val insisted as she offered a weak smile. "Chance spent the better part of the morning beating himself to a pulp for missing the symptom all these years."

"Shouldn't Shane be taking medication or something?"

Val shook her head. "Maybe. Maybe not. You can bet Chance will have him tested every which way to make sure he gets whatever treatment is necessary. He's not in any immediate danger. There are different types of Von Willebrand's. Shane has the most mild form. It would only be a problem if he had surgery and the surgeon didn't know about the condition, or…"

"Or what?"

"He has children with someone who also carries the gene."

Taylor did her best to absorb the information. "So, if Shane has it, does that mean his brothers have it, too?"

Val gave her a straight look. "That's the million dollar question, isn't it?"

"WHAT THE HELL IS THIS?" Shane demanded as his brother brought the SUV to a screeching halt. The headlights of Seth's vehicle joined those of three other cars, cutting through the inky darkness to illuminate the front of the bunkhouse.

The marked police cars, lights strobing red and blue against the worn wooden building, sat idling, their doors open, officers hunkered down, weapons drawn.

Seth reached over, opened the glove compartment and gave Shane a hand gun. The weapon felt smooth and slightly cool in his grip as he checked the chamber and the magazine. He tasted bitter adrenaline just as one of the younger officers weaved his way over to the SUV.

"Adams is holed up in the bunkhouse."

"Why didn't I hear this on the radio?" Seth barked.

"Just happened," the deputy explained. "We went inside to arrest Adams and then, well, all hell broke lose. Everyone was filing outside all orderly and everything, then the foreman goes after Adams and the next thing we know, Adams has a gun and he's holding it to the foreman's head."

"Will? Will is inside with Luke Adams?" Shane demanded.

The deputy nodded. "Adams told us all to get out or he'd blow the guy's head off."

"Get on the radio and alert the state police," Seth instructed. "I want this area cleared of everyone who doesn't need to be here."

"I can do that," Shane said as he rushed from the truck. He crouched, zigzagging his way to the closest ranch hand half-hidden behind a nearby tree. "Get all the men out of here," he said.

"Will's in there with that lunatic," the man argued.

"We'll handle it. The last thing I need is a shoot-out. I want everyone out of here. Now. Make it happen."

The hand did as instructed. About two dozen men worked their way along the fence line, using the trees and fence posts as cover.

Shane's every nerve was on high alert.

Through a small window, he could just see the top of Will's head. He felt a surge of anger tempered by uttered helplessness. There wasn't a lot he could do about the former, but the latter was assuaged by clicking off the safety and loading a round into the chamber of the gun in his left hand.

Shane was desperate to help his friend. Maybe he should have brought Taylor along. Not that he wanted her in harm's way, but perhaps she could offer suggestions, a way to talk Adams out of the bunkhouse without Will, or anyone else, getting hurt.

Seth joined him then, pressing his shoulder against the trunk of the pine tree. "There's a hostage negotiator on the way. He'll be here in an hour."

"An hour?" Shane repeated, infuriated. "What are we supposed to do until then? Ask everyone to take a sixty-one minute time-out for pie and coffee?"

"Wait him out," Seth replied as he used his thumb to dial his cell phone.

The sound of the bunkhouse telephone ringing incessantly cut through the night. Will moved out of his line of sight as the ringing went on for almost two minutes, before Shane heard some muffled arguments from inside, followed by a crash. Then there was silence.

"Must have yanked the phone off the wall," Shane guessed. "I say we rush the place. The son of a bitch has already killed a woman in cold blood. Do you think he'd hesitate to kill Will if it would do him any good?"

He felt Seth's fingers close on his upper arm. "I know how much Will means to you, but we're going to do this by the book."

"I'm not going to do anything stupid, but I need to do *something*," Shane argued. "Let me go in, Seth. Maybe I can—"

He was silenced by the blast of a gunshot.

Shrugging off his brother's hold, Shane raced to the bunkhouse, right on the heels of three deputies in bulletproof vests. In tandem, the officers kicked in the door, splintering the wood near the lock as they trained their weapons on the interior.

As he'd been taught, Shane kept his elbows flexible as he stared down the barrel of his own gun. After a quick scan of the room, he focused on Will.

His friend was standing over the body of Luke Adams, a small-caliber revolver dangling loosely between his thumb and forefinger.

A handful of officers swarmed the long,

narrow room. Shane breathed in the acrid scent of gunpowder as he strode toward Will. As expected, the older man showed no emotion as he said, "Didn't have a choice."

Shane nodded as he glanced briefly at the blood pooling from beneath the lifeless body of Luke Adams. "You okay?" he asked, knowing it was rhetorical, since Will would never admit to being hurt.

"I'm fine."

Seth joined them then, asking, "What happened?"

Will took in a deep breath and leaned back against the footboard of one of the unmade beds. Shane and his brother also moved out of the path of the incoming paramedics.

"The kid went off," Will answered, rubbing the day's worth of graying stubble on his chin. "Got the call that the law was coming for him, so I came to keep an eye on him."

Shane tucked his gun in the back of his waistband as he listened to Will. As always, the foreman's voice was devoid of emotion as he recounted the events.

"The cops burst in, and the next thing I knew he had a revolver stuck in my ear." Will paused, looking down at the weapon he was holding before handing it over to Seth. "I'm pretty sure that's one of my guns, too. Kid musta stole it from my desk."

"How come you didn't recognize him leaving Webb's Market?" Shane asked. "Seems to me you should have known it was Adams when you saw him running away after he killed Doris."

Will shrugged. "Happened really fast, and like I told Seth, here, I only caught a glimpse of the guy from the back."

"You didn't know your gun was missing?" Shane asked, perplexed since it wasn't at all like Will to be so cavalier with a weapon.

"It's calving season," he said. "We've been putting in twenty-hour days."

Shane listened, wondering why the explanation didn't ring totally true. It was crazy, since he'd known Will practically all of his life. If Will told Seth that's what happened, then that's what must've happened. Shane's brain knew that for a fact. Yet his gut was telling him differently.

Crazy was a good adjective to describe the way Detective Rollins looked when he burst into the bunkhouse. His eyes were narrowed and it was clear he was angry as hell.

"What part of 'stay out of the investigation' don't you understand, Sheriff Landry?"

Shane watched as his brother responded to the question with something akin to boredom. "How do you figure this was part of your investigation?"

Rollins glanced over at the body, then glared daggers at Shane. "Oh, Luke Adams was a big part of my investigation."

"How so?" Shane asked.

"He called me a few hours ago," Rollins answered. "Claimed he had information on the murder of your parents. He wanted to make a deal."

"He was playing you," Shane retorted. "Probably realized he was about to be arrested for the Webb's Market robbery-homicide."

"Adams claimed he was being set up on that," Rollins argued. "Said you Landrys were framing him just like you framed his father."

"His father?" Shane repeated, not following at all. He turned to Seth and asked, "Know anything about that?"

Seth shook his head, but Will cleared his throat and said, "It was a long time ago."

"What was a long time ago?" Shane asked, an odd feeling rumbling in the pit of his stomach.

Will shifted from foot to foot. "The thing with his old man. Adams is a pretty common name, so I didn't put it together when Luke signed on."

"What happened to his father?" Shane asked.

"Caleb had me fire him," Will stated. "Jack was the accountant here. He was siphoning money from the ranch. Stole nearly fifty grand before your dad and I discovered what he was doing. After that, the guy couldn't find work anywhere. Last I heard he was drowning himself in the bottle."

"When was this?" Shane demanded.

"Thirty-plus years ago," Will answered.

Chapter Fourteen

"Did you sleep?" Shane asked when he stuck his head in the doorway to the office.

Taylor was seated at the desk, totally focused on the computer screen until she glanced up. Her breath caught when she saw him. Even in the middle of a disaster, Shane had the uncanny ability to paralyze her just by showing up.

His still-damp hair was pulled neatly into a ponytail. His expressive blue eyes showed just a hint of the strain of the previous night's activity. But it was his broad, bared chest that sent her heart racing.

All instincts begged her to jump out of her chair, run into his arms and spend the next several hours in his bed. Luckily though, her brain was in charge and not her libido. Well, mainly in charge, she admitted privately when she felt a shiver of desire ripple through her.

"I slept a little," she said, waving him over. "Come look at this."

Shane finished buttoning his shirt as he came around the large desk, then placed his hands on the back of the chair. It creaked under his weight as he leaned forward. His face was next to her ear, his warm breath tickling her neck. He smelled of heat and soap.

She had to give herself a little mental slap. This was not the time to be sidetracked by her physical fascination with this man. Then there was the added pressure of having knowledge of his blood tests before he did. She felt an odd mixture of emotions, a need to protect him from the truth struggling against her innate need to be honest with him. She wished now that she hadn't learned of the results first. Sometimes ignorance truly was bliss. Not that he'd be ignorant of the facts for long; Chance planned on telling Shane in the morning. Despite her argument that he be informed right away, Chance had wanted to do his research before he told his brother. He'd pointed out that twenty-four hours wasn't going to make any difference at this point. But they both knew Shane would demand to know everything there was to know about his illness. Chance wanted to have all those facts to give him. She would just have to keep the secret to herself for another eighteen or so hours.

Squeezing her eyes shut for the second it took to clear her thoughts, she said, "This is a fairly complete life history of the late Luke Adams. Well, as much as I've been able to cobble together so far."

"And you did this because…?" he asked.

She scooted to the side, thrown off her concentration by his closeness. Heat practically radiated from his large body and the scents of soap and shampoo filled her nostrils. Taylor was glad he couldn't read her thoughts. If he could, Shane would know that she really, *really* wanted to drag him down the hall to her bedroom and spend a lazy day in bed. She almost smiled. *Bed* and *lazy* were two words that didn't go together when thinking of Shane.

"Taylor?" he prompted, placing his hand on her shoulder and giving a gentle, prodding squeeze.

"Right. Sorry. Well, I got to thinking after last night. Why would Luke Adams go to all the trouble of getting a job here, then blow it by robbing the market and killing Doris?"

"Because he's a career criminal?" Shane suggested, moving around so that he faced her as he leaned against the edge of the desk. "You heard Seth and Detective Rollins. Luke started getting into trouble when he was in his late teens."

"But before that," Taylor pointed out, "he was an Eagle Scout."

"People aren't born bad," Shane remarked dryly.

"No," she insisted, "I mean that literally. He was an Eagle Scout. Look at these articles." She started handing him the pages she'd printed out. "Luke was only fourteen when he made Eagle Scout, which, by the way, is an accomplishment and a half. That was the year before your parents' murder and six months before his first arrest. Something bad must have happened to make such a great kid go down the drain so suddenly."

"You're analyzing a dead guy, you know that, right? A dead guy who killed Doris and would have killed Will had Will not wrestled the gun away from him."

Taylor nodded. "Yes, and I know that Rollins found a prepaid cell phone on Luke and that the memory card in the phone proves that phone was used to make the threatening calls to me."

Shane rubbed his freshly shaved chin. "What's your point?"

"It's too strange," she argued. "I told you I met Luke."

"Yeah?"

"He didn't know who I was," she stated emphatically. "I had to tell him I was the housekeeper. So why would he call to threaten me if he didn't even know who I was?"

"Because he was a criminal?"

She glared up at him. "Think, Shane. Luke was here the day I went up into the attic. If he was some crazed killer, that was a perfect opportunity for him to rampage."

"But he had the cell phone, and preliminary ballistics on the gun prove that it was the one used to kill Doris. Pretty compelling if you ask me."

"Here." Taylor shoved a sheaf of papers into his hand. "Read what I printed," she insisted. "Luke was an above-average kid. Good grades, basically model behavior. Something happened to change him."

"That would have been about the time that his father was outed as a thief," Shane mused. "Will told me that even though no charges were filed, Jack Adams was a pariah after that. Started drinking, couldn't get a job, lost his house. Something like that would certainly change a kid's behavior."

"Speaking of that," Taylor said, her fingers flying over the keyboard as she spoke, "the father, Jack, made the papers a few times. Disturbing-the-public charges, mostly during court hearings regarding his son."

"Pretty fatherly behavior."

"Yes, but look at this quote," Taylor said, pointing toward the computer screen. "According to the reporter on scene, a very drunk Jack called the judge corrupt. Said the whole system was flawed and unfair."

"I think I said something similar when Clayton was convicted of killing Pam." It was clear Shane was only half listening as he riffled through the pages she'd printed. Clearly not impressed, he set them on the desk beside his hip. "Outbursts like that aren't all that uncommon in the heat of the moment."

"Okay. For the sake of argument, let's say it was nothing more than an emotional rant by an alcohol-impaired parent. It still doesn't change the facts. And another thing. Did you know Luke's mother and Doris were friends?"

That seemed to get his attention. His dark brows drew together. "And we know this how?"

Taylor shuffled some papers around until she found the old photograph. "This was taken at the Hunt Club the year before you were born. This…" she paused to tap one of the faces in the picture "…is Leona Drake. At least that's the name Doris gave me. I did a computer search and found that Drake was Leona's maiden name. She was married to Jack Adams and they had a son, Luke."

"Obviously, they knew my parents," Shane said, running his thumb over the aged image.

"Correct. When I spoke to Doris, it sounded as if she and Leona were pretty close friends, which would mean Luke knew her as well. So why did he kill one of the only people in Jasper he had a history with?"

Shane frowned. "So what are you saying here? That there's some sort of connection between Luke killing Doris and the death of my parents? That seems like a helluva stretch. Do we know for a fact that Luke knew Doris?"

"One way to find out," Taylor suggested. "The father is still alive. I could go see him."

Shane started shaking his head. "No way, I'm not letting you go see some drunk alone. I'll—"

"Just make him crazy," Taylor interrupted. Closing her hand over his, she said, "If he started drinking because your father fired him, do you really think he'll be in a hurry to talk to *you?*"

"No."

"I'll go this afternoon, before my class."

"No way, Taylor. You are not running all over hell and gone by yourself."

"So come with me," she suggested. "But you have to wait in the car. No, make that completely out of sight. Killer or not, Luke was still his son and he's a grieving father."

"I hate the idea. A lot. But okay. You're better equipped to handle him."

She shot him a suspicious glance. "Are you making fun of me, Shane Landry?"

He reached out and cupped her cheek. His palm was warm and she reflexively leaned into his touch. "I'm complimenting you, Taylor. That's what a person does when they care about someone."

She stiffened. "Don't do that."

"Compliment you? Or care about you?"

Taylor scooted as far away from him as possible, until the chair rolled to a stop against the bookcase. "The latter."

The smile he offered was sad and caused a tightness in her chest that made her feel as if she'd just kicked his favorite dog. "Let's not do this now, Shane."

"Okay."

She hadn't expected such a quick and amicable surrender. Tilting her head slightly, she regarded him for a few seconds. The man was sneaky.

She scowled. "Just 'okay'? No argument?"

He shrugged. "I'm willing to hold off on the full court press."

She relaxed a little. "Good."

"For now."

Not good.

BY MIDAFTERNOON, Shane still wasn't back and Taylor was feeling pretty antsy. She was staring at the photograph, hoping for some sort of divine inspiration. All the faces were familiar at this point, even if the picture was more than three decades old.

Grabbing the telephone, she called directory assistance, then had the phone company automatically dial the office of Senator Brian Hollister. It was a long shot and she knew it.

Hollister was a very popular elected official whose main claim to fame was carrying the torch of the common man into politics. Taylor navigated through a maze of administrative personnel before reaching the senator's personal secretary. Vaguely, she recalled meeting her—a petite woman with bright green eyes and a pretty smile—at the Landrys' funeral.

"May I tell Senator Hollister what this is in reference to?' she asked.

"I'm calling about Caleb and Priscilla Landry."

"Please hold."

A few minutes later the senator's assistant came back on the line. "Senator Hollister is in a meeting at the moment. Would you like to make an appointment to see him—"

Taylor almost groaned. Of course the senator was busy. What had she been thinking? That he'd drop everything because she called? Waste his time reminiscing over old pictures? Still, she had to try. Something about this picture niggled at her brain. "I appreciate that. But it's imperative that I speak to him as soon as possible."

Anticipating that the senator would see her in oh, about three months, Taylor impatiently listened as the woman's fingers clicked on her keyboard, apparently checking her boss's calendar.

"I have June 19 at ten o'clock or July 8 at three-thirty…."

"Neither," Taylor told her firmly. "It's vital that I see the senator, or at least talk to him, today."

"That's not—"

"Please. It could be a matter of life and death."

"The senator has a break between a luncheon and a meeting at two-fifteen. Would two o'clock this afternoon suit you, Miss Reese?"

Taylor glanced up at the clock. If she left now, she could just make it. "Yes, thank you."

After she hung up, Taylor tried several times to track Shane down. He wasn't in the barn or up at the calving shed. None of the hands could tell her when anyone had last seen him, only that he was with Will. And, damn the man, he still wasn't answering his cell phone.

She left him a message on his voice mail. Just to be on the safe side, she also scribbled a note for him and left it on the table.

Contacting Shane was just a matter of courtesy, Taylor thought irritably as she quickly changed clothes for her meeting with the senator.

For reasons she did not want to analyze, she was ticked off that Shane seemed to have walked off the edge of the earth without telling her where he'd gone. Perhaps because they'd been on such high alert for days—first with his parents' bodies being found, then the threatening phone calls, and then Doris's murder. She'd quickly become used to having him there watching out for her. Silly to feel the loss now.

While there were still dozens of questions to be answered, there was no longer any threat of danger. Luke was dead. Shane wasn't obligated to tell her where he was every minute of the day, and she didn't need to feel strangely abandoned and vulnerable.

The drive to the office of Senator Hollister gave her time to think. Canyon Creek was north of Jasper, a small community at the edge of Helena National Forest. Following the deserted black ribbon of macadam, she tried to organize the fractured bits and pieces into something that made a little more sense.

"Luke couldn't have killed the Landrys, he was only seven when they disappeared. Then there was the money," she murmured. "The hundred thousand dollars withdrawn from the account by Caleb Landry the day they disapp— *died.*"

Fishing around in her purse, Taylor found her cell phone, placed it on the console as she attached the ear bud, then pressed Sam's speed dial number. His secretary put her through directly.

"Hi, Taylor, everything okay?"

"Fine," she insisted, filling him in on her plans for the day.

"Shouldn't you have waited for Shane?" Sam asked, his tone conveying genuine concern.

She was touched by how much Sam—heck, all the Landrys—cared for her well-being. "He was tied up and the senator only had a limited window of time. Listen, have you found anything relative to the money yet? Anything suspicious or strange?"

"One thing. Doesn't make a lot of sense, though."

"What is it?"

She heard the shuffling of papers before Sam said, "Beginning in 1978, there were large, semiannual withdrawals made from my parents' savings account."

"Shane would have been ten," Taylor remarked. "That was around the same time your mother took him for the blood test."

"I know. There's got to be a connection."

Shoving her hair off her face, Taylor asked, "Any thoughts? Theories?"

"Chance is trying to track down a nurse who worked at the medical center where Shane had the test. Maybe she can shed some light on why Mom waited until he was that old. I mean, if she knew her…*lover* had this disease, I don't understand why she'd wait all those years to have Shane tested."

"I know," Taylor agreed. She had an odd feeling as if she was missing something right in front of her. "I never knew your mother but I saw the records she kept on Shane. She didn't strike me as the kind of woman who would let a potential medical issue go ignored. Especially not for ten years."

"I did know her," Sam said. "And I'm having trouble accepting the fact that she cheated on my father."

Taylor heard the blend of pain and anger in Sam's tone. It would be ten times worse for Shane. "What about before then? What about the money stolen by Jack Adams? Did your father or Will keep the proof that he was embezzling from the ranch?"

"Yep," Sam answered, followed by the sound of more papers being shuffled. "For an accountant, Jack wasn't very swift at covering his tracks."

"What do you mean?"

"Let's just say that if I was going to steal from my employer, I would have done a better job of it."

"Give me an example." She turned north on Highway 279, adjusting the visor as blinding, bright sunshine streamed into the car.

"The ranch has a general operating account as well as several investment accounts. Jack was a signatory on all those accounts. The unauthorized withdrawals were from the general operating account."

Taylor's brow furrowed as she tried to follow

the gist of the conversation. She wasn't very successful. "Does it matter which account he stole from?"

"If you don't want to get caught, it does," Sam scoffed. "Back then, the bank sent monthly statements on the operating account to the ranch. Meaning Jack risked getting caught every thirty days."

"And the investment accounts?"

"Quarterly statements," Sam answered. "Easier to hide discrepancies that way."

"An accountant would know this?"

"Definitely. It's pretty basic stuff."

"So why did he do it?"

"I have no clue," Sam admitted. "I've been over this paperwork a dozen times and I can't find a pattern of any kind."

"Does that matter?"

She heard Sam expel a breath. "Normally, yes. If Jack was behind in his mortgage, you'd expect money to disappear at a set time every month. If he was gambling, the withdrawals might coincide with weekends. The theft in this case was pretty random."

"Why wasn't he arrested?" Taylor asked.

"I can only guess at this point. I can't find where the money went and I've got computer resources my dad didn't have at his disposal back then. I'm sure Dad ran into the same problem. It's hard to prove someone is a thief if you can't trace the money to them."

"But if he was the accountant…"

"*Knowing* someone is a thief and proving it are often two different things, Taylor. So far, I can only prove that the money was transferred to Western Union."

She felt hopeful for the first time in the conversation. "Wouldn't they have a record of some kind? A receipt, something?"

"No. Basically, Western Union gets the funds, then the recipient can go to any one of their authorized locations and claim the money."

"So it's a dead end?"

"I didn't say that," Sam said. "At the time of the embezzlement, there were only five authorized locations in Montana. I'm working that angle now."

"That's good, right?"

She heard him expel a long breath. "Only if the stolen money was picked up in Montana. If Jack had it sent out of state, I'm not sure we'll ever know what happened to it."

"Are you coming over in the morning?" Taylor asked, feeling her stomach knot just thinking about Shane's response to hearing the news.

"Of course. He's going to need you, Taylor."

"I...it's a family thing. I don't want to intru—"

"He needs *you*," Sam stated simply. "You're going to be there for him, right?"

Her heart pinched in her chest and her next breath was something of an effort. "I think he needs his brothers more."

"No, Taylor. *You'll* be the one he'll want."

Chapter Fifteen

The offices of Senator Hollister occupied the first floor of a three-story building in the center of Canyon Creek. It was a small, well-manicured town dependent largely on tourism and a relatively famous drug rehabilitation center.

It was midafternoon when Taylor parked her car on the street about a block away from the office and strode toward the brick building.

She had to pass through a metal detector guarded by a young, uniformed officer, then a second set of glass doors before she was greeted by a pretty redhead wearing a headset.

The office smelled faintly of popcorn. The walls were lined with framed articles tracing Hollister's unlikely rise to relative fame.

"I'm Taylor Reese," she informed the smiling woman. "The senator is expecting me."

"Have a seat, Miss Reese. Can I get you come coffee, tea, a bottle of water?"

Taylor shook her head, thanked her, then watched the twenty-something woman disappear behind a door marked Private. When several minutes passed, Taylor began to grow restless. Lacing her fingers, she stood up and moved around the reception area, reading the articles that traced the history of the senator's career.

Hollister wasn't your typical career politician. In fact, he wasn't a politician at all, but a used-car dealer. Well, according to one article, that had been his focus until he'd gotten annoyed by a zoning issue and thrown his hat into the ring. The rest, as they say, was history.

Running as a regular guy willing to shake up the career politicians, Hollister had won his senate seat by the narrowest of margins. His constituents had latched on to Hollister's claims that he was one of them. According to one reporter, Hollister's rough-around-the-edges appeal negated the reality that he was a lousy businessman who had filed for bankruptcy twice before running for office.

His best asset was his wife, Elizabeth. One article even hinted that she was the brains behind the man's carefully orchestrated upset victory.

Taylor inched between two wing chairs in order to get a better look at the attractive woman waving from the front page of a news article. The color image was very flattering and very familiar.

Slipping the attic picture out of her purse, Taylor compared the unnamed woman to Hollister's wife, Elizabeth. They were one and the same. Pleased with her detecting skills, Taylor stuck the picture back in her purse.

The redhead returned then, wearing an apologetic smile. "I'm sorry, Miss Reese, the senator is on a conference call."

Checking her watch and doing a little math, Taylor said, "I can wait for a little bit."

"He may be awhile."

Taylor shrugged and sat on the edge of one of the chairs, grabbing a magazine and flipping—disinterestedly—through the pages. Five minutes passed, then ten, then twenty. He was pretty lackadaisical for a guy who only had a few minutes between appointments. Pressing her palm against her knee, she was attempting to stop the agitated tapping of her foot when her cell phone rang.

"Hello?"

"Please tell me you didn't go to Canyon Creek by yourself," Shane said with mild irritation.

"I didn't go to Canyon Creek by myself."

"Good. Where are you?"

"Canyon Creek."

He sighed for effect. "Do you really think it's safe for you to be running around alone?"

Taylor looked up to find the receptionist openly listening to every word. Placing one hand over the mouthpiece, she met the other woman's curious gaze and said, "I think I'll step outside so I don't disturb you."

Grabbing up her purse, she walked out to the street. "Luke is dead, remember?"

"Luke didn't kill my parents, remember? Seth is sending a deputy to follow you back to Jasper. I'll see you at home."

"I haven't seen the senator yet."

"I suggest you hurry it along because the deputy will be there in about a half hour."

"You sound annoyed."

"I was annoyed when I saw your note. I've moved past that to completely pissed, but we'll have that conversation when you get back here. I've got someone at the door, so we'll talk about this later. Bye." The line went dead.

She should have known there'd be hell to pay for going off on her own, but listening to his even, clipped syllables made her wince. For good reason, too.

Flipping the phone closed, she headed back inside, wondering when she'd gotten stupid.

And it was stupid to drive all the way up here alone. Any number of bad things could have happened.

So why did I do it? she asked herself as she cleared the metal detectors for a second time.

Because if I can't be with him, at least I can help him.

And look what I did. she continued the mental lashing. *Like my mother and grandmother, I willingly put myself in physical danger for a man.* Her shoulders slumped. Obviously, her life plan wasn't working. She was making decisions—bad ones—based on a man.

It didn't matter that he was a terrific man, or that he was in trouble. All Taylor could think about was the chilling reality that being in love, acknowledged or not, had made her reckless.

Five minutes after her return to the waiting area, Senator Hollister opened the restricted access door and greeted her with a broad grin and a very enthusiastic handshake. So enthusiastic that her hand stung as she allowed him to guide her down the narrow hallway to his private office.

Thirty years ago, he'd been a thin, pencil-necked twenty-four-year-old. Now he was a silver-haired man with capped teeth and a sparkling pinky ring in the shape of a bear. When he sat behind a large, glass-topped desk, she noted that the bear's eyes were made of small garnet chips that glowed demonic red in the sunlight streaming through the window.

His cologne was a heavy, musky scent that Taylor actually tasted as she sat in one of two large, black leather chairs opposite the desk.

"If I'd have known you were such a pretty little thing, I wouldn't have kept you waiting," Hollister said, his brown eyes narrowed when he grinned.

Taylor didn't take offense. Instead, she ignored the inappropriate tone and content as just a generational difference. In her experience, men over fifty didn't always get that women her age loathed that kind of comment. "Thank you."

"My secretary said you have a picture you want me to look at?"

Nodding, Taylor pulled the photograph from her purse and slid it across his cluttered desk. The minute his brown eyes fixed on the image, his smile grew taut, almost forced. "Such a shame," he murmured.

"What?"

"Caleb, Priscilla, Doris, Leona," Hollister sighed. "Hard to believe they're all gone now."

"Did you know the Landrys well?"

Hollister lifted his shoulders. The action caused his double chin to press against the too-tight collar of his stark white dress shirt. "Not really. I mean, we all belonged to the Hunt Club. There were parties there almost every weekend." He shoved his cuff back to look at his watch, not bothering to be subtle. He was a busy man, granting a favor, and he clearly didn't want her to forget it. "Hell," he said with a small smile, "in the sixties, there were just parties, period. Know what I mean?"

Taylor smiled back. "What about Jack and Leona Adams? What do you remember about them?"

"Leona was a pleasant gal. Her husband was quiet. Pencil pusher type," Hollister said with a derogatory little sneer. "Sorry to cut this short, Miss Reese, but I have a meeting." He stood and came around the desk. "Thanks for stopping by," he said, holding the photograph in her direction. "If I can be of further help, you just give a call, okay?"

"I would like to know more about the—"

"I'm sorry, but I really don't have any more time today," he said, moving to the door and grabbing the knob.

Reluctantly, Taylor started past the senator, feeling very much as if she was being hurried along. He was in a serious rush to get her out of his office.

As she was leaving the building, Taylor practically fell into Mrs. Hollister as the older woman came charging up the stairs.

"Excuse me," Taylor said.

Elizabeth Hollister didn't exactly exude warmth. She was a thin, drawn woman who looked much older than her fifty years. A thick, chunky necklace clattered against the buttons of her suit as she brushed imaginary cooties from the front of her blazer.

"Are you okay?" Taylor inquired.

"I'm fine. You're the Landrys' maid, aren't you?" She started nodding her head, her brown eyes narrowing slightly. "I vaguely remember you from the funeral."

"Yes, I work for the family."

"What are you doing here?" the senator's wife asked.

Actually, it sounded more like an accusation, which caught Taylor a little off guard. "I stopped by to see your husband."

"Well then, I'm sure he was helpful." Elizabeth started to walk away.

"Since you're here, is there anything you can remember about the people in this photograph?" Taylor called, whipping it out of her purse and holding it up.

"I remember it was a long time ago," Elizabeth replied, after glancing at it briefly. "Beyond that, you'll have to excuse me, Taylor."

Taylor? "But—"

A split second later, Taylor was alone, listening to the sound of her own voice echo off the building. She considered chasing the woman down, but then remembered that Elizabeth was the wife of a senator, and the deputy sent to follow her back to Jasper was pulling up to the curb behind a dark blue pickup truck.

Immersed in her own thoughts, Taylor barely mumbled the appropriate pleasantries as she was escorted to her car. The Hollisters were strange. And she'd bet her Ph.D. that they were hiding something. But what? And how had a woman who "vaguely" remembered her from the funeral several weeks ago know her first name?

The obvious guess would be that Hollister was Shane's biological father. If her suspicions were true, why hadn't the senator come forward and said anything to Shane in all these years? If it was true, did Elizabeth know? And if so, why didn't she toss him out on his senatorial ear?

"And why," Taylor asked out loud, "are all the people in the photo dying violent deaths?"

Taylor was no closer to an answer when she

stuck her hand out of the car window and waved off the deputy as soon as she reached the driveway to the Lucky 7. As she went up the lane she noticed that he waited until she'd come to a stop in front of the house before he drove on. She cut the engine and grabbed her purse.

It was already close to four, and she suddenly realized she wasn't even remotely prepared for her evening class. Calculating prep time, the visit to Jack Adams's place and the drive to campus, she wondered if she'd be able to do it all.

Almost at a run, she pushed open the front door, closed it behind her and started down the hallway to her room. She almost didn't see him there in the shadows. It wasn't like Shane to sit in the living room. Taylor knew instantly that something was very, very wrong.

"Welcome back," he said, his intonation completely flat.

"What's wrong?" she asked as she flipped on a light.

It seemed as if Shane had aged five years since breakfast. He was sitting on the sofa, elbows on his knees, his shoulders slouched and his chin resting in one hand. His gaze was distant, his mouth bracketed by deep lines, his brow furrowed and that little muscle at the side of his jaw tensed.

A fist tightened around Taylor's chest as she walked into the living room. "Shane?"

He patted the cushion next to him and waited until she sat. When she did, she noticed him pressing the heels of his palms against his eyes. "Detective Rollins came to see me this afternoon."

Her heart skipped a full beat. "And?"

"It's all there, in black and white." He indicated a neat stack of papers in the center of the coffee table. "I had to haul Chance out here to explain it all to me."

"What?"

"Let's see." He began ticking things off on his fingers. "There's no way I'm Caleb Landry's son. The up side to that is I may not be the killer. According to Detective Rollins, they can't make a one-hundred-percent match of my blood to the blood on the towel that was recovered with the bodies because of the age and poor quality of the evidence. But I do have the right blood type, so I can't be excluded, either."

Dread filled her. "And?"

"And I have a hereditary genetic disorder."

She wanted to take him in her arms and

comfort him. Instead Taylor reached out to give his shoulder a gentle, reassuring squeeze. "I'm sorry, Shane."

"Nothing I can do about it," he said numbly. "This Von whatever-it-is disease isn't deadly, so I guess that's something."

"Of course it is," she insisted. "I looked it up, and so long as you take precautions before surgery, or if you have a bleeding episode, it won't impact your life one iota."

His brows arched as he fixed his gaze on her. "Looked it up?"

Taylor sucked in a breath. Bad. Very, very bad.

"What were you doing? Thumbing through a medical dictionary? Why would you be looking up a disease no one has ever heard of?"

Damn it. She'd told Chance not to wait to tell Shane. Now look at the position he'd put her in. Shane was never going to understand this. And who could blame him? "I went to see Chance yesterday. He gave me a crash course on platelet disorders."

"You knew about this?"

Shane felt completely out of control, as if his life was one big wave about to crash onto shore. Knowing Taylor had kept such an important secret from him didn't exactly help.

She grabbed his hands, holding them tightly in hers. "I didn't say anything because it wasn't my place."

He cast her a sidelong look. "A hint would have been nice. Better than hearing it from a detective."

"I know," she agreed. "I'm sorry."

"That helps," he remarked sarcastically as he expelled a breath. "I don't understand why you would keep this secret, Taylor. Wait, that's a theme for the day, isn't it? I don't know why my mother had an affair."

He stood and started to pace, needing some way to release the explosive nervous energy knotting his insides. "Know what I did when the detective was explaining to me that my father wasn't really my father, and 'oh, yeah, you have a disease'?"

"That's an awful way to find out something like this. What did you do when he told you?"

"I got mad," Shane admitted. "Then I felt guilty about being mad."

"Normal reaction. Often when a person—"

He paused and glared till she fell silent. "I don't want to be analyzed, Taylor. I want to understand all this. How could my mother have cheated? Did my father know? Maybe that's why the two of us clashed. Maybe I was a walking, talking reminder of his wife's infidelity. And the big one. Who *is* my father?"

"Caleb Landry was your father in all the ways that matter, Shane. I have a feeling when you're not overrun by conflicted emotions, you'll see that clearly."

Taylor twisted a lock of hair between her thumb and forefinger as she continued, "People have affairs for all sorts of reasons."

Shane massaged his tense shoulders. "Well, I'm not like you, Taylor. You're fine with not knowing who your father is. Hell, you're comfortable with anything so long as it doesn't have any strings attached."

His words hurt more than she thought possible. "That's not fair, Shane."

Lifting his head, he met her eyes. "Really? You're so good at ascribing motives to other people. Ever turn that mirror on yourself?"

"I'm comfortable with who I am."

"No, Taylor, you hide from who you are. From what you feel." He blew a breath toward his forehead. "We've lived together for too long. Know how I know?"

Mutely, she shook her head.

"'Cause I actually get you. You don't choose not to love me, you don't know how. If you did, you would know that when someone you love has been given some pretty devastating news, you offer comfort, not analysis."

"I'm trying to be comforting," Taylor argued. "I spent the afternoon running all over creation just to gather information that could help you."

"It would have been nice to have you here," he told her honestly. "I needed you, Taylor. Not Will or Chance or anyone else. You."

His brother had been right. Shane *had* needed her. "I had no way of knowing that Detective Rollins would come here. I don't know what else I can say or do."

"And that's the heart of the problem, isn't it?"

"It doesn't have to be a problem, Shane. You're making it one."

"Then we shouldn't have made love."

Her eyes narrowed angrily. "Convenient of you to decide that after the fact. What a...a *man* thing to do."

"No, Taylor, that's the problem. I'm the only one here interested in a relationship. You're just jerking my chain until you have your diploma in your hands and you can be on your merry way without a backward glance."

"Well, you got the jerk part right. You promised me that you wouldn't do this again."

He balled his fists at his sides. "Do what?"

"Lash out at me because you've had some unpleasant news."

"Unpleasant?" he mocked, astounded by her understatement. "Swallowing a bug is unpleasant. Discovering you don't know who your father is falls under a completely different heading. Tack on knowing that your biological father murdered your parents and dumped their bodies down a well to rot takes it to a different level, wouldn't you say?"

She folded her hands neatly in her lap. "I'd say you have every reason to be confused and emotionally fractured."

"You going to charge me for this office visit?"

"What do you want me to say?" she snapped. "I'm really, really sorry this happened. I'm sorry you found out this way and, well...hell, I...probably do...love you."

"Well, I'm sure basking in the warm glow of that proclamation of love."

"It's the best I can do," she insisted stiffly.

"You know something, Taylor? The sad truth is, I agree with you." He willed himself not to walk over to punch a gaping hole in the wall. But he sure wanted to hit something. He wanted some way to alleviate the crushing emptiness in his chest. Anything that wasn't an analysis of his motivations.

Oddly enough, as devastating as it was to hear the news of his parentage, it paled in comparison to knowing that he had no future with Taylor. Nothing that would leave his sanity or his heart intact. That much was brutally clear.

Walking to the coat rack, he snapped up his jacket, turned to her and asked, "Coming?"

"Where?"

"I'm going to see Jack Adams. While I'm there, maybe I should ask if he's my father."

"Then of course I'm coming," Taylor replied, scurrying off the sofa, grabbing her own jacket and fairly chasing after him down the front stairs.

Chapter Sixteen

It wasn't until Taylor had her second arm in its sleeve that it dawned on her she had said the words to him. *I love you.* And nothing. No response, no whoop of joy, no…anything. Nada, zero, zippo. Granted, her timing sucked, but never in her wildest dreams had she ever considered that if and when she said those weighty words, they'd be tossed off like an unwelcomed insult.

The late afternoon air couldn't hold a candle to the chill in the air inside the SUV. Taylor guessed she should do something to smooth things over. After all, the man, obtuse moron that he was, *was* in crisis.

She winced, glad he couldn't see her face in the dull glow of the dashboard lights. *He's right. I do make everything sound clinical. Lord, life was a lot easier when we were limited to playful, pointless banter and I didn't have to weigh the importance of every word.*

"Off the subject," she said facetiously, "I understand your anger, Shane. You're hurt, and you feel betra—"

"Do *not* reduce what I'm experiencing to one of your textbook cases. Yes, I'm hurt by this, and damn it to hell, *yes*. I do feel betrayed that you— *all* of you—knew this and kept it a secret." He put a hand up when she tried to talk. "I understand that Chance wanted to present me with all the facts. Intellectually I get it, okay? I get it.

"Just give me a second here to assimilate everything I've learned. In the meantime, why don't you tell me about your visit with Senator Hollister?"

He wasn't going to talk about the elephant they'd left back in the living room. Fine with her. She had a little adjusting and assimilating of her own to deal with. She recounted her visit to the senator's office. "He couldn't get me out of there fast enough. Any ideas why?"

"Not really. I barely know the guy. I remember him coming by from time to time, but that was way back, around when he opened his second used car lot. Mostly I just remember that Hollister ran these really cheesy TV commercials in the middle of the night."

"He likes playing the good old boy. What else do you know about him?"

"What I read in the papers. Married to Elizabeth, who used to be known as Lizzy until she clawed her way up the social ladder."

"I met her as well," Taylor said. "She wasn't what you'd call warm, either."

"Rumor has it Lizzy's from one of those old Southern families. The grandfather made a few millions—textiles, I think. The money only lasted one generation, leaving Lizzy and her cousins in the position of having to make it or marry it."

Taylor nodded. "That fits. Is that how she ended up with Hollister?"

"Sure. I think she was probably still in her late teens when she married him. My guess is that she was facing college or the secretarial pool, so Hollister and his used car empire must have looked pretty damn good to her."

"So, they knew your parents? Socialized with them?"

"*Knew* might be a little strong," Shane murmured. "The Hunt Club was Jasper's version of a country club. If you paid the annual dues, you were a member."

As he continued to speak, the tension in his voice lessened. There was still an edge, but not as pronounced. "I remember my parents talking about the parties they used to attend, but that ended when I was still in elementary school."

"Why? Did it close down?"

"It's still open," Shane said. "I haven't been there since my ninth birthday. My...dad took me there to do some skeet shooting."

She felt a stab of pain, hearing him stumble over the reference to Caleb. She was respectfully quiet for a moment, then asked, "And not after that?" In the dark, without seeing his face, she could tell that Shane was thinking the same thought.

"My mother took me for the platelet test not long after that."

"Okay," Taylor mused. "So, we know that something happened when you were ten years old that made your mother get you tested. Were you sick? Anything?"

"No."

"Why then? Why wait so long?" Taylor still had that nagging feeling she was missing something, an integral piece just there, out of reach. It was frustrating as sin. But it was easier to hone her thoughts on who'd killed the Landrys than to delve into her feelings. Lord knew they were a jumbled mess. Mostly of her own doing.

Where was her all-powerful life plan when she needed it most? "Maybe Jack Adams can tell us."

That seemed very unlikely a half hour later when Shane turned down a rutted, overgrown road. Road was a generous description. It was more like a trail, complete with deep gulleys and small boulders that had to be negotiated like a giant slalom.

Dust sprayed in through the air vents, causing her to taste dirt as the car rocked and lurched up the steep incline. It was dark as pitch and Taylor still didn't see any signs of a house.

"Are you sure this is the right road?" she asked.

"Yes. According to Seth, there's an old cabin about a mile back from the main road. He failed to mention that the road was this rough."

"I'm getting a bad vibe about this," Taylor said, feeling the hairs on the back of her neck prickle. "Maybe it isn't a good idea. His son just died. He probably won't welcome the intrusion."

"I don't think Jack Adams even remembers he had a son named Luke. The way I hear it, the guy's been living inside a bottle of cheap Scotch for years."

"Look! Look!" Taylor cried, pointing at the shadowy outline about fifty feet ahead.

As impossible as it seemed, the house was in worse shape than the road. The wood exterior was cracked and several of the logs hung askew. The roof was patched with a rusted slab of corrugated aluminum and the windows were so dirty that they absorbed the beams from the headlights.

There was an odd smell, offensive and sweet all at once, and very strong as soon as they exited the car. "What's that?" she asked, bringing her jacket sleeve up to mask her mouth and nose.

"Poor housekeeping?" Shane suggested wryly. Leaving the car lights on, he slammed his door and strode toward the shack, Taylor hot on his heels. "Hello? Anybody home?"

There were no lights inside. No movement, no nothing, not even after Shane pounded on the door for several seconds.

Fear shot through Taylor as she crept over to a window and tried to peer inside. She had to step over a heap of assorted debris, bricks, twigs and other things she was sure she'd hate seeing in the light of day. Grimacing, she used her sleeve to clean a circle of glass. The interior grime was too thick for her to make out much beyond the vague images of a table and chairs.

"I don't think he's here," Taylor said.

Shane whipped out his cell phone and a few seconds later was speaking to Seth. The conversation lasted a minute or two. When he finished, he turned to Taylor, his face pinched in a frown. "Seth checked with Detective Rollins and apparently no one has been able to find Jack Adams. A fact Rollins failed to share. The state police have been by here a few times."

She spotted something by the front door. Something that appeared fresh, new and very out of place. "That explains this," Taylor said, reaching down and gingerly picking up a crisp, white business card with the state police emblem embossed on it. On the back side, someone had written, "Please contact us immediately." Showing it to Shane, she added, "Tough way to find out your child was killed in a hostage standoff."

Shane reached for the door handle, feeling the cold knob turn easily in his grasp. "Mr. Adams?" he called.

"We can't just go in," Taylor grumbled as he shoved the door past a high point on the floor that caused it to scrape and stick.

"Mr. Adams? Jack?" Not getting any answer, and fully aware that lots of folks in Montana shot first and asked questions later, he felt for Taylor and tucked her protectively behind him.

He listened for sounds of life, but there was nothing but the gentle rustling of the trees and distant cry of a wolf.

"We shouldn't do this," Taylor repeated, though he didn't hear the same sense of conviction in her tone.

Groping along the inside wall, he found the switch plate and flicked on the light. A single, naked bulb dangled from the ceiling. The harsh glare blinded him for a second as the smell of stale cigarette smoke filled his lungs.

Once his eyes adjusted, Shane surveyed the sparse, single room cabin. There was a small, round kitchenette table with three chairs. All the seat cushions were split, most having been repaired with rope or duct tape. One chair sat at an angle to the table, as if someone had pushed it back to stand up.

Shane's conclusion was further supported when he walked over and smelled the remnants of the nearly empty glass. "Scotch," he confirmed.

Taylor was still plastered to his side. Not that he blamed her; the cabin was creepy and dank and generally nasty. It was also deserted. Glancing around, Shane cataloged the contents as Taylor's hold slipped from his waist. A camp stove, crusted with baked-on gunk, sat on the chipped counter. Shane placed his palm on top of a small, dorm-size refrigerator and felt no vibration from the motor. Maybe the bad smell was coming from inside the unconnected appliance. He decided not to check.

He looked up to find Taylor crouching beside the unmade, metal twin bed. She picked up a small, framed photograph. "This must have been his wife, Leona."

Shane murmured some sort of acknowledgment as his eyes darted around the room, looking for something, anything. A clue of any kind would be welcome at this point. He had no idea what he was searching for, or if it was large or small. Jack Adams lived a spartan life. In addition to the kitchen and bedroom areas, the only other furnishings were a lumpy old recliner and a small, tin tray table holding a twelve-inch black-and-white television with a wire coat hanger and tinfoil rigged as an antenna. There wasn't a drawer in sight. Nothing to rifle through.

Dingy, graying paint and plaster were chipping off the wall. A large, moldy water spot on the ceiling drew his attention to the far corner. To a narrow door.

"A closet," he said, as if he'd discovered the New World.

"What are we looking for?" Taylor asked as, with a grimace, she got down on her hands and knees to peek under the bed.

"It'll jump out at us when we find it."

"If *anything* jumps out from under this bed, I'm back in the car."

He was still grinning as he opened the closet door. The narrow enclosure had a single clothes rod and a single shelf holding two boxes. Four plaid shirts hung on hangers and a large pile of dirty laundry was shoved into the corner. Okay, he wasn't touching that, either. A pair of worn hiking boots sat on the floor.

Shane reached to the shelf, grabbing first one box, then the other, and placing them on the bed for inspection.

Taylor stood, flipping her hair back and dusting her palms on the edge of the sheet. She grimaced and shivered. "This is a vile place."

"You can take a long bath when we get home." He was lifting the flaps of the box when he stopped abruptly and looked at Taylor's flushed face. "You missed class."

She shrugged and reached across to slide the second box closer to her side of the bed. "It isn't like I'll get detention or anything."

Tilting his head, he watched her briefly, trying to remember the last time Taylor had skipped a class. Never. Not once in five years. He'd seen her drag herself out of a sickbed to drive several hours in a blinding snowstorm. That Ph.D. was the most important thing in her life. But tonight, now, when he needed her, she'd bailed without so much as saying boo.

For a few seconds, he allowed himself to believe that she'd done it because she actually did love him. In that small amount of time, his heart sang. The heavy pain of the day's disclosures vanished at the mere thought that Taylor was capable of loving him the way he wanted her to. The way he needed her to. The way he loved her. Then he gave himself a little mental reality check.

The temptation to take whatever crumbs she tossed his way was strong. But in the end, he needed more. A lot more. He needed her to feel what he felt. The blinding, white-hot, intense kind of love like…well, like he'd seen his parents share.

Shaking his head, Shane brought himself back to his now strange world. Caleb wasn't his father and the marital relationship he'd so admired his whole life was, apparently, a sham. That didn't change the fact that he was responsible for his parents' death, albeit indirectly. That was the only logical conclusion in light of the DNA results. So, following logic, his biological father was the killer. Why? If he could answer that, he could come to grips with himself, his brothers and his future.

His maudlin thoughts were interrupted by a triumphant little sound from Taylor. "What is it?" he inquired.

Slowly, she ran her fingernail along the edge of an old wedding album she took from the box. "There's something behind the cardboard."

Moving quickly, Shane went to her side, helping support the album as she coaxed two envelopes out from behind a photograph of Jack and his new bride. "What made you look behind the picture?" he asked, trying to fill the time as she took great care not to tear the photo.

"See the outline?" she replied.

In fact, there was a ghostly image, roughly the size and shape of a standard envelope, creased into the picture. "I probably would have missed that," he admitted.

"My grandmother did the same thing," Taylor said. "She used to hide money in frames behind my annual class pictures."

"Good a place as any, I suppose."

"A relatively safe place. The kinds of men she brought home weren't really the family type—oh, wow!"

"Wow is an understatement."

The papers were bank statements. Based on the postmarks, she knew they had been mailed to the Lucky 7 when Shane was roughly fifteen, three years before the Landrys were killed. One was addressed to Caleb and Priscilla Landry and the other was for the general operating account. "Why did Jack have these and why did he save them?" she wondered as she opened the envelopes, removing the statement and the canceled checks.

"This is from my parents' personal checking account," Shane said, examining the checks in turn. "Feed and Seed, Webb's Market, Guy's Pharmacy, Feed and Seed, Amanda Grayson, Cash—"

"What?" Taylor interrupted, trying to snatch the checks out of his hand.

"Cash," Shane repeated. "My mother wrote this check. It's for five thousand dollars."

"No, not that one. The Amanda Grayson one."

Shane sorted backward until he found the check. "Here it is—Amanda Grayson, twenty dollars."

Taylor checked the memo section. "Hunt Club?"

"Probably some sort of fund-raiser," Shane suggested, going back to the checks. "Yes.

That's gotta be it. Here's another one two weeks later. Amanda Grayson, twenty bucks."

"Amanda Grayson would not belong to the Hunt Club. She wouldn't help with a fund-raiser."

"I told you, it was a social thing, too."

Fervently, Taylor shook her head. "I don't care if they were raffling off a night in Buckingham Palace. I'm telling you, Mrs. Grayson would not support a hunt club. She's staunchly antigun. Trust me, Shane, I've worked with Mrs. Grayson for two years and I know with every fiber of my soul that the woman would not be involved with anything even remotely related to ammunition, targets, guns or weaponry of any kind."

"Okay," he agreed. "But that's a forty dollar thing, Taylor. Look at this. In one month my mother paid out five grand from her personal account and another five grand from the operating account. Both payments are to cash." He handed her the checks. "See?"

The checks were identical. *Too* identical. "I need light."

"For what?"

"Bring that stuff."

Without waiting for him, Taylor went outside and sucked in a deep breath of much-needed fresh air. Going to the front of the SUV, she placed the check Priscilla Landry had written from her personal account against the warm, bright light of the headlamp. The light made the check almost transparent. Then she overlaid the second check, the one from the general operating account.

"I think I know how Jack Adams embezzled money from your family."

Shane leaned beside her, his breath warming her neck in short bursts as he looked more closely. "He traced my mother's signature? Not very high tech."

"He traced the amounts, too," Taylor said, seeing how perfectly the script matched. "Basically, Jack used your parents' personal checking account as a guide for what to steal and when to steal it. These two checks are a month apart, so I'd bet that if we compared all the checks, you'd have irrefutable proof of Jack's theft almost down to the dollar."

"So, Jack was a thief. And his son is a killer? But Jack couldn't have killed my parents because Detective Rollins already verified that he was in prison doing six months on a drunk and disorderly charge. Luke is on videotape killing Doris, but Luke couldn't have killed my parents because he was in juvenile hall at the time. So we can prove that they are both criminals, just not the *right* criminals?"

Taylor nodded grudgingly, rubbing her chilled arms. Bugs flew in and out of the beams from the headlights. "Pretty much." She turned and leaned against the car, utterly frustrated. When Shane reached for the checks, his fingertips brushed her palm, sending a small shiver up her back.

Slowly, she looked up into his hooded gaze. She swallowed once, twice, waiting anxiously as a kaleidoscope of raw emotion swirled in his eyes. Tucking the checks into his shirt pocket, he slipped his hand inside her jacket, resting it on her waist. He lifted the other to her face, gently caressing her cheek with the pad of his thumb.

Shane wasn't the only one whose thoughts and needs were jumbled and confused. Taylor wasn't handling her own inner turmoil too well. His mouth was inches from hers as his gaze flickered between her eyes and her mouth, finally settling on her lips. Fear, longing, anticipation—all of it pooled together into a consuming puddle in her tummy.

Pressing her palms against his chest, Taylor fully intended to stop anything before it started. Not that she didn't want his mouth on hers; she did. Desperately. But this was neither the time nor the place. Except that her rational mind kicked in a fraction of a second too late. Far too late.

All she needed was the feel of his rapidly beating heart beneath her hand and all her good intentions evaporated. The sensation of his thighs pressing against her became the focal point for her desire-addled brain. He smelled warm, inviting and familiar. His touch made her feel safe and…loved.

Getting up on tiptoe, Taylor tried to press her mouth to his. Shane deftly shifted his position, leaving her standing against the cool metal grill of the car.

"No more."

"No more what?" she managed to gasp, wondering when her voice had turned so whiney and pathetic.

He dug in his pocket for the car keys. "No more sex, Taylor. We're done."

Chapter Seventeen

The dashboard clock read quarter to eight when Shane called Sam and gave him the updated financial information they'd found at the cabin. It was pretty amazing to listen via the speakerphone as the Landry brothers agreed on which bank official to summon back to work. Power definitely had its advantages.

As did compassion, loyalty, kindness and many, many other attributes Taylor could assign to Shane. It was very dark, but as she sat in the passenger's seat, she finally saw the light. A scary, thrilling, wonderful light. Crispy, clearly, unequivocally.

She'd spent her whole life planning how *not* to include a man. So she'd never actually thought about her life *with* one. She'd never considered what it would be like not needing to be with him but *wanting* the experience. Choosing it.

And not her mother's choices, either. Not bad ones. Not necessarily safe ones, but the kinds of chances you have to take when your heart is as involved as your head.

Glancing over at Shane, Taylor was practically bursting with the need to share her epiphany. She took a deep breath. She even opened her mouth, but nothing came out. The words, the feelings, jammed in her throat, too powerful, too all encompassing to verbalize.

This was the scary part and it would pass. Then she could tell him that she really did love him. Really, truly.

And he'll believe me this time…why?

Euphoric, her heart pounding as adrenaline raced through her, she fell back against the seat. How was she going to regain his trust? How was she going to convince him that she was utterly sincere? And how could she even begin to describe this feeling of lightness? This feeling of…*rightness?* Taylor felt giddy with her self-realization.

"You're quiet," Shane said.

Not inside I'm not, she thought dryly, as her mind raced. "I'm thinking." Thinking about their future possibilities like a butterfly flitting over a flower garden. She glanced out at the bright, even slashes of white as they drove beneath the lampposts through town.

"About the murders? Me, too."

Okay, I can change gears. For now. "Let's stop by the Hunt Club. Will it be open?"

"Should be."

"That place is the only common denominator in all this."

"Maybe. Or it could just get us another piece that doesn't fit. I thought you'd want a bath after Jack's place."

"Two baths. But right now I want information more."

He reached out and rested his hand on her thigh. It was just enough to keep a flicker of hope alive. She entwined her fingers with his, her heart waiting for a reciprocal gesture. Without looking at her, Shane turned his hand over and held hers.

The breath Taylor had been holding eased a little.

Baby steps.

The Hunt Club was a large, two-story building with a smattering of cars parked in the lot. Trucks, more accurately. Taylor recognized some of them and mentally went about matching people to vehicles while Shane selected a spot to park.

He didn't take her hand again once they exited the car. Taylor felt a chill run through her as they walked on the gravel path toward the club. The twang of a country song blared a greeting when Shane opened the door and escorted her inside.

She was as acutely aware of his hand at her back as she was of the dozen or so pairs of eyes tracking her. No wonder they called it a "hunt club."

A large, utilitarian bar, dotted with bar stools, spanned the length of the room. Only three were occupied. She recognized one man from town but couldn't recall his name, so just smiled.

"Hey, Shane, ma'am," the bartender began with an uncomfortable smile. "Sorry, but it's still a private club. Members only."

"We just dropped by for a little history lesson. That okay?" Shane asked easily.

The thin man shrugged and slapped two napkins down on the thickly varnished bar. "Whatta'll you have?"

"A beer and…?"

"Red wine," Taylor stated, slipping up onto a stool. "How long have you been serving here?"

The bartender placed a glass of wine in front of her, then opened a long-neck bottle of beer for Shane. "Monday, Wednesday and Friday for the last twenty years."

Taylor swallowed her disappointment along with a sip of her wine. "Is Amanda Grayson a member?"

His brow furrowed as his graying brows drew together. "No, ma'am."

"Ever been a member?" Taylor pressed.

"Not as long as I've been around. I think she tried to get a permit to picket us once. Something about the annual turkey shoot contest being cruel to birds." He snorted. "She's probably one of those who thinks the turkeys in the grocery store died of natural causes."

"I believe her objection was that the contest is on a family holiday and there's often more drinking than hunting." Taylor's back stiffened as she defended her friend. "Alcohol and family stress can be a bad combination."

"Thanks for the tip," he said, wandering off to wait on another customer.

"When did you become the Jasper Temperance League?"

She sighed. "I'm not, really. I just happen to agree with Mrs. Grayson on that issue. People do stupid things when they're drunk."

"More wine?" Shane teased.

"When they drink to *excess*."

"So?" He rested one foot against the boot rail and said, "This field trip is turning into a total bust, don't you agree?"

"No I don't. Look. There. Behind the bar."

"Trophies? So what? Lots of local clubs sponsor sports leagues."

"How many are co-sponsors with Hollister Motors?" She reached out and grabbed a fistful of his shirt. "Follow the years, Shane. Hollister Motors and the Hunt Club co-sponsored teams until 1978."

"The year my mother took me in for the blood test. The last season before my father stopped bringing us here to shoot."

"There has to be a connection."

"Hollister is a freaking senator, Taylor." Shane struggled to keep his voice at a whisper. "If the connection is Hollister—and that's a big *if*—why would he kill my parents? By default, that makes him my biological father, and I can't believe he'd have risked his political future on a child he obviously didn't want. Play it out to the end. If Hollister was my mother's...*married lover,*" he spat the words, which left a bitter taste in his mouth, "he'd have every reason to want to keep it a secret. Killing them doesn't accomplish that goal. Fast forward fifteen years, and now explain to me how he can be involved in any of the weird stuff that's been going on.

"First it was the calls and the note stabbed into your car seat. Hollister is too public a figure to be running around town with knives, taking potshots at you."

"Probably."

"Definitely," he insisted. "He lives and works in Canyon Creek. You tell me how he got Luke to fake a robbery in order to kill Doris. How did he turn Jack into a thief? I'm starting to wonder if all these events are even connected. And what does any of that have to do with a blood disorder my own mother didn't know I had until I was ten years old?"

"*Because* she didn't know you had it."

Shane gaped at her. "Huh?"

Taylor slipped off her stool. "Hurry up and pay. We've got to go see Amanda Grayson."

A few minutes later, they were on the road again. It was getting late by ranching community standards. Most people were up with the sun, so anything after 10:00 p.m. was considered an all-nighter. High headlights, from a truck following a reasonable distance behind, were bright enough that he automatically adjusted the rearview mirror to cut the glare.

Taylor gave him directions, then Shane

called the ranch to check in. The latest update was a half-dozen new calves. He was sure Will was pulling his hair out, but Shane knew the man never balked at hard work. "The birthing barn must be crazy with activity," he said. "I guess at some point I'll have to talk to my brothers about, well, about my taking care of the ranch and…"

"Don't be a jerk. Do you honestly think one blood test can change the way they feel about you?"

"I don't know."

"Sure you do," Taylor retorted. "What if the shoe was on the other foot? Would you turn your back on one of your brothers?"

"No."

"Then have some faith. And turn at the next corner."

AMANDA GRAYSON TUGGED at the edges of her robe. Her long gray hair was braided, dangling to well past her waist as she led them into the kitchen of her modest home.

"I'm glad you're here," she said, filling a teakettle and placing it on a burner. "This has been weighing on me for some years."

"You've been expecting us?" Taylor asked.

Her smile was warm but tempered with

sadness. "Not you," she said, then turned her eyes on Shane. "You."

He was slightly taken aback as he took the seat she offered. "Why me?"

"I've been holding something for you. Something from your mother."

Shane felt his stomach drop into his toes. "And you never got around to giving it to me?" He reached out for Taylor's hand, comforted by the feel of her fingers lacing with his.

"It wasn't my place, Shane. I made a promise to your mother that I felt ethically bound to keep."

"She was murdered."

"Which made my position more difficult," Amanda said as she hobbled over to a drawer next to the stove. Removing a sealed envelope from the drawer, she presented it, saying, "Take this into the other room. Taylor and I will have some tea."

He hesitated for a second, then squeezed Taylor's hand before taking the thin envelope. He had it opened by the time he settled into a chair.

The letter was several pages in length, all written in neat precise script, dated February, 1986:

Dear Shane:

I wanted you to hear the truth from me sooner but I never summoned up the courage. Now, if you've found your way to Amanda's doorstep, she can help me tell you all the things I was never brave enough to say aloud.

You'll be eighteen in two weeks. The last of my sons to hit that milestone. I'm very proud of you, Shane. We both are. Your father and I love you very much. No matter what, never question that.

I want only good things for you and your brothers. Most of all, I want you to be as happy as I am at this moment. I need you to know that you boys and Caleb are how I define myself. Not what happened eighteen years ago. Don't let it define you, either. Even if I could change the past, I wouldn't do it, not if it meant not having you in our lives. Neither would your father.

Before I say anything else, think back, Shane. Remember all the good things. Separate your conception from your life. That's what your father and I chose to do, and we're so glad.

Okay, so now for the hard part… We

were attending a party at the Hunt Club. I went outside for a breath of air when it happened.

In those days, we didn't have words like 'acquaintance rape.' All I knew was someone grabbed me, threw a tablecloth over my head. I was attacked and it was over. I stayed outside for a while, trying to figure out how to tell your father.

You know his temper. I understand now my feelings of shame were normal. But that night I was shocked, embarrassed, scared, angry, and all I could think about was going home to my children. I didn't want anyone to know what had happened. Especially not your father. I know it wasn't my fault, but it was a different time, Shane. Not like now.

I didn't see my attacker's face that night, but his voice was familiar. He was a friend of your father's. I didn't know how to handle it. So I hid. From everyone, including your father. I didn't say anything to him, not even after I found out I was pregnant. I've never been ashamed or sorry about you, Shane. Not for one second.

I'm not sure how, but I kept my secret. It wasn't like I intended to deceive your father or you. At first I was ashamed, then afraid, and then one day it didn't matter anymore. You were our beautiful baby boy.

I can tell you it wasn't something I consciously thought about. Not for years.

Then when you were about ten, I got a phone call. I recognized the voice. It wasn't the man who attacked me, but he knew all about it. I didn't believe him at first, but then he told me about this strange blood disease and told me to have you tested.

I should have gone to your father immediately, but I didn't know how. I did take you out of town to a doctor, who explained the disease and swore to me you had a very mild form that shouldn't affect your life.

The man who called me was having some financial difficulties, so I gave him some money, hoping that would be the end of it. That went on for about a year. I finally broke down late one night and told Caleb what happened, but not that I'd been paying money to keep my secret.

I was braced for his temper. Instead, your father kissed my forehead, then went into your room and kissed you as well.

It never mattered, Shane. You were— you are—our son. I know that doesn't change what I did, all the lies that have come home to roost, but I never intended for anyone to get hurt. Least of all you.

Last night I told your father about the money. He's really mad at me—you know him. He pretty much dared anyone within earshot to call you anything but his son.

We're going to fix this money thing, Shane, and then your dad and I will sit down and talk with you. I hope when all the dust settles, you'll understand why I made the choices I made.

Love, Mom

A lump the size of China clogged Shane's throat as he wiped tears off his cheeks with the back of one hand. His emotions ran the full gauntlet from anger to sorrow and back again.

His body felt drained as he rose and walked toward the kitchen.

"Can I get you something?" Amanda asked.

"A name," Shane said, astounded he was capable of making the request sound reasonable. He wasn't feeling very reasonable.

"I don't know his name." Mrs. Grayson pursed

her lips and shook her head. "All I know is that Priscilla said the man she was paying worked on the ranch."

Chapter Eighteen

"Hollister worked on the ranch," Taylor said later when Shane careened into a parking space near the sheriff's office. "He told me so when I met with him. It has to be Hollister."

"I've got my own plan for getting a blood sample," Shane said, smashing the heel of his palm against the steering wheel.

"I don't think this is a *good* plan," she cautioned. "Talk it over with Seth. Then do it legally. If we're right, and it is Hollister who's been behind all this, you want the man punished, don't you?"

"There is no 'if,'" Shane said, his tone grim. "Trust me, he will be punished."

"I don't think it's a good idea for you to go off half-cocked," she stated as they reached the entrance.

The dispatcher, seated with her feet on the desk, straightened when they burst inside.

"Seth's on his way. Said for you to wait if you got here first."

"Just great," Shane groused.

Watching him was like watching a wounded animal looking for a target. "There's a vein threatening to explode in your temple," Taylor said softly. "Take a deep breath. This will all be resolved soon."

"I'll be calm a few minutes after I put my fist through Hollister's teeth."

"Very manly," Taylor said dryly. Grabbing his arm, she shot a men-will-be-men smile at the dispatcher, who was watching them. "But there are much better ways…." She tugged him into Seth's office and closed the door, then pushed him into one of the visitor's chairs. She nodded at the closed door. "She'd make a wonderful witness for the prosecution. Take that deep breath. Seth will be here soon."

Shane jumped up and started pacing his brother's office like a caged lion. "I just want to do this. I owe it to my mother's memory."

Taylor turned her chair a little so she could watch him. She sympathized with his impotent rage and frustration, but he *couldn't* go off half-cocked. They'd prove that he hadn't killed his parents, but if he assaulted Hollister, there'd be no going back. "She'd probably like it more if you didn't go to jail in her name. Do this inside the legal system."

"I'll take the sheriff with me. Seth can legally watch me pummel the guy into hamburger. Satisfied?"

She opened her mouth just as the door burst open. "Saved by the cavalry."

"Let's go," Seth said shortly.

"Hello? What about…me?" Taylor said into the echoing silence after the door slammed behind the two brothers. They had taken off, oblivious to everything and everyone.

Taylor was panicked. Raking her fingers through her hair, she thought for a minute, then grabbed the phone and dialed Sam. She told him what she knew and asked for his help. "It's not that I necessarily care what happens to Hollister, but I don't want Shane ruining his life."

"I'm on it, Taylor. You stay put."

That should have been reassuring, but she still had a nagging doubt swirling in her head. And nothing but time on her hands. Time that was moving so slowly she actually flicked the clock twice just to make sure the hands weren't stuck in place.

The television and VCR were still in Seth's office. Taylor cued the tape and started playing and rewinding the footage of the robbery. With each pass, she struggled to find even one more detail. The robbery was the one element that didn't quite fit. Assuming Hollister was guilty, how was he connected to Luke?

"He isn't," she murmured. At least there wasn't any connection she could find. She tried expanding her search of the videotape. Other than taking up thirty minutes of her time, she didn't learn anything new, so she went back to the few frames that she thought depicted the shadow of a second person reflected on the dairy case.

"Jack, maybe?" she wondered. He was unaccounted for; he was a drunk and a thief. It fit. Except that Jack couldn't have killed the Landrys, and that was the key.

"Or the Hunt Club is the key," Taylor argued, feeling a little silly that she was debating with herself in a closed, empty room. "Or Shane's paternity is the key. Or—" The phone rang, making her jump. "Yes?"

"Will's here," the dispatcher said. "He says Shane told him to take you back to the ranch."

How typical of Shane to think of her in the middle of all this. "Thanks, I'll be right there." Feeling completely thwarted by her lack of progress, Taylor shut off the television and the VCR and left the office.

She was out on the street, uttering a third, effusive apology to the craggy cowboy, when she saw something that made her stop dead in her tracks. There, idling at the curb, was a dark blue pickup truck. Strobelike, a series of images flashed in her brain.

"I know this truck," she murmured. "It's—"

"Courtesy of Hollister Motors," Will said, jabbing a gun against her rib cage. "Get in."

The door swung open and Taylor found herself staring into the cold, narrowed eyes of the occupant who'd been shielded behind the vehicle's tinted windows. "You've been a real pain in my rear end, Miss Reese. But we're going to rectify that now."

Right outside the sheriff's office, Taylor was lifted off the sidewalk and dumped onto the pickup's bench seat. Senator Hollister sat on one side of her, while the ranch foreman quickly slipped in the driver's side and closed the door.

"You?" she demanded of Will. The bitter taste of fear-inspired adrenaline coated her tongue. "Both of you? Together?"

"We're a team, aren't we, Will?" Hollister asked, chuckling softly.

"What are you? Jasper's version of Leopold and Loeb?" She winced when Hollister's elbow caught her in the cheek.

They were headed back toward the ranch. Which made no sense. The place was crawling with people—many of whom were Landrys. She chewed her lip as Will drove the speed limit out of town.

"Curious, aren't you?" Hollister mocked. "Why the ranch? Well, I happen to know that at least two of the Landry brothers are on their way to Canyon Creek. I know this because Will tells me everything, don't you, buddy?"

Again, the cowboy said nothing, though Taylor felt his body tense where their shoulders touched.

"He doesn't have a choice," Hollister continued. "Will did a bad thing years ago, so now Will has to do whatever I ask him to do, right, Will? If he doesn't, he goes to jail for a long, long time."

"Really?" Taylor asked, buying time to think. "What bad thing did Will do?"

"He got very drunk one night at a party. So drunk that he didn't remember what he did until I reminded him."

"Shut up, Hollister!" Will growled. "We've got enough trouble. She doesn't need to know all this."

A scenario was falling into place in her mind. "A party at the Hunt Club?" she asked.

"Yes." Hollister's tone wasn't quite as confident. "Very good, Miss Reese."

Yes, she thought. Almost as good as committing a sexual assault and then convincing some poor drunken sap that he was responsible. "Why go back to the ranch?" Taylor asked.

"You tell her, Will. Tell her how you've been holding out on me all this time."

"Money's there."

"What money?" she asked.

Hollister leaned over, placing his vile mouth very near her ear as he said, "The money Priscilla Landry was supposed to cough up the night I killed her. With everything that's happened, I'm going to need all the traveling cash I can find."

Taylor wiggled closer to the driver. "If she was paying you off, why kill her?"

"That wasn't the original plan," Hollister explained. "See, thanks to Will's...*indiscretion* and the resulting birth of the youngest child, I should have been able to feed from the Landry *trough* well into my golden years. Like I told Will, he put that tablecloth over her head so she'd never be able to identify him. And hell, she'd pawned off the youngest as a true Landry, so she wasn't going to put up a fuss. The Landrys were like our own personal ATM until

Priscilla had an attack of conscience and spilled everything to Caleb."

"Still doesn't explain why you killed her," Taylor said, seeing the lights of the ranch up ahead. As their destination grew closer, the bubble of panic in her stomach got larger and larger.

"Why, once Priscilla told Caleb, we didn't have a choice. Will would have been arrested, and that Caleb—he was a vindictive son of a bitch—he would have tracked me down, too, because of my financial interest in the matter."

Taylor was torn between her fear and a burning desire to take her shoe off and beat Hollister bloody. As tempting as that was, it didn't solve her immediate need. Staying alive did.

"There's no money at the house," Taylor pointed out. If there was a large amount of cash, she'd know.

"Tell her, Will."

"There is," he admitted.

"Yes," Hollister agreed, scratching the lower of his two chins with a small-caliber handgun. "I've forgiven Will for holding out on me all these years but he's promised to turn the money over to me in exchange for Shane's life. I'll take this money and what little I could get from my personal accounts and be on my way out of the country."

Will parked the pickup in front of the house. Taylor realized she had to get Will on her side, and to do that she had to break Hollister's hold on him. Unfortunately, she was pretty sure the senator would shoot her before he let her finish a sentence. "Let's go get my money, Miss Reese. Then I can watch you die."

Not if I watch you first, she thought as she slowly climbed the steps to the door, the two gun-wielding men flanking her. There had to be something she could use to her advantage. *Think. Think. Think.*

"Where to?" Hollister asked.

"Money's in the attic," Will answered.

No it wasn't. She'd been through every box in that attic. Nothing was making sense except the certain knowledge that she'd be dead in a matter of minutes if she didn't do something. Fast.

Her eyes darted around the foyer. The only thing between her and the staircase was the hall table. It held nothing more sinister than a house key and lamp. So, she reasoned as she pretended to stumble, something was better than nothing.

She palmed the key and kept moving. The

edges weren't at all sharp, but she kept it hidden just in case an opportunity presented itself.

Hollister was breathing heavily by the time they reached the bottom rung of the attic ladder. "Him first," he said, yanking Taylor back so that she was sandwiched between the two of them. He rammed the gun into the small of her back as Will started to climb.

"WAS THE DISPATCHER positive?" Shane asked his brother again.

"Very."

"Will told her all this? Word for word? In, like, sixty seconds?"

Seth heaved a deep breath. "He told her to watch until the car pulled away. She did that."

"It was Hollister? She's sure? Because it's really dark out."

"For the hundredth time, yes. She saw his ruby pinky ring, the one with the bear head that he wore in all those dumb-ass commercials. Will said that as soon as they drove away, she was supposed to call and tell us the killer was going back to the ranch."

"How does Will know about Hollister?" Shane asked.

"We can ask him in about five minutes if

you'll shut up and let me drive. I know you're worried about Taylor. We'll get there. Nothing will happen to her."

"She's with a killer, Seth. She isn't safe."

The car was still rolling to a stop when Shane leaped out, rounded the pickup and bounded up the stairs. Carefully, he eased open the front door and tried to detect any sounds over the pounding of his own pulses. Nothing. Nothing. Yes.

Stealthily, he climbed to the second floor, reaching the hallway just in time to see Hollister's foot disappearing up the ladder into the attic.

"Wait." Seth was just behind him, chambering a bullet into his gun.

Waiting was not an option. Not when Taylor was in danger. Shrugging off his brother's cautionary hand, Shane started up the ladder.

Hollister had Taylor by the hair, roughly shoving her toward a pile of boxes. Shane had barely processed that bit of information when he realized Will also held a gun. His first instinct—beyond the one telling him to rip Hollister's spleen out through his nostrils—was to call out. Until it sank in that Will had his gun trained on Taylor, not on the senator.

Taylor was on her knees, rubbing the back of

her head with one hand and cringing as she waited for Hollister to put a bullet in her brain. Then she saw it—a brief, beautiful flash of movement. Shane.

Her heart practically leaped out of her chest. "Since you're going to kill me anyway," she began, slowly working the pointed end of the key between her third and fourth fingers, "maybe now is a good time for me to tell Will he isn't a rapist."

The second she had the last syllable out of her mouth, she ducked and rolled, using her momentum to plant the key deep into Hollister's thigh.

"What?" Will yelled.

Then the room exploded, literally.

Hollister was falling backward, his leg wound bleeding like a geyser, but his finger squeezing the trigger of his gun. Wood splintered; bullets ricocheted. All Taylor knew was there was no way on earth she was going to let an evil Hollister or a misdirected Will have a second chance at destroying the Landry family.

Stretching to her very limit, she made a fist and punched the key deeper into Hollister's leg. He yelped and cursed, and then Shane's large body was sailing through the air, falling on top of the larger, older man.

She counted one more gunshot before being blanketed in an eerie silence.

Taylor half crawled, half lunged to Shane. There was so much blood. "Are you hurt?" she screamed, rolling him over and touching him everywhere.

"No. You?"

He started at her scalp and worked his way down, scanning anxiously. Other than a slight bruise on her cheek and some wood fibers in her hair, there didn't seem to be anything wrong with her. He was finally able to breathe.

Shane devoured her mouth, lacing his fingers into her hair as he tasted her lips, her cheeks, her eyelids. "You're crying," he murmured, tasting the salty remnants of a tear.

"Delayed stress reaction."

He groaned. "I don't want the clinical explanation, Taylor. I was thinking along the lines of something more personal."

"Um, Shane?" Seth said, his voice somberly echoing off the attic walls.

Hugging Taylor to him, Shane glanced over and saw Will slumped against the wall. A bullet, either Hollister's or Seth's, had found its way to him.

Dipping his head, Shane said a silent prayer for his friend's redemption. He had no such charitable feelings for Hollister. The senator was still bleeding from his leg. His face had gone stark white and his breathing was shallow and labored.

"Go call an ambulance, okay?" Shane told Taylor, kissing her forehead.

Then he removed his shirt and crouched over Hollister, pressing the fabric to the semiconscious man's leg.

Her throat suddenly felt thick with unshed tears. "You're a good man, Shane Landry."

He rose, helping her to her feet. "If he lives, he'll do so knowing that I gave him life and not vice versa."

She got up on tiptoe and kissed his chin. "You're an *exceptional* man."

"I am," he said, patting her behind.

"You'll make some woman a fabulous husband," she called over her shoulder.

"Are you asking me to marry you?"

"Maybe."

Epilogue

"Dr. Taylor Reese." She beamed as she read the nameplate Shane was affixing to the side of the freshly stained wooden building.

Thanks to him, it had taken less than six months to get the place refurbished and opened. It was a perfect, perfect day. The sun was shining, the trees glowing with rich golds, greens and yellows. The furniture was in. The wallpaper was up. Everything was done. She was official.

Shane draped his arm over her shoulders. "So, is it the way you imagined?"

"Better," she exclaimed, squeezing him tightly. "There's privacy and yet it's still, technically, in town, so people will come. We have a playroom for children and a real computer system for me. Nothing could make this any better."

Well, that wasn't completely true, but close

enough. As in the six months they'd been working on the building, Shane hadn't once said he loved her. Not even now that she said it freely—heck, *hourly*—to him. He'd been a regular saint, too. Dodging almost every one of her attempts at seduction. Of course, Shane had two secret weapons—Sam and Callie's twins. Since Sarah and Kasey had arrived, Shane used the babies like shields to keep her at bay.

Nuzzling his chest, she breathed in his scent and smiled. He'd cave. She knew it. He'd already stared to crumble. She tested her theory, dancing her fingertips along his spine just to change the rhythm of his breathing. Worked every time. She could be patient. She didn't want to, but she could.

"We should probably go get the ribbon you're going to cut for the grand opening," he said.

"I have a new couch. We could take it for a test drive—ouch!"

He swatted her fanny and looked down to see the sparkle in her hazel eyes. She was happy. That mattered, a lot. She was happy with him. That mattered more. "You're a Ph.D. now, Taylor. You can't proposition me on the street anymore. It isn't professional." He went inside and returned with a bag. "Per your request, a large red ribbon across the entrance for the grand opening."

It was like watching an old woman on Christmas morning. Taylor carefully removed the ribbon from the bag as if she was going to save it for posterity. Did women reuse opening-ceremony ribbons? he wondered, amused. He managed to maintain his cool for a little while, then lost patience. "Sometime before we grow old is fine."

"This is really big for me, Shane. I'm savoring every moment. I'm going to look back on this day when I'm ninety, and I want to remember every…"

He'd never heard such a deafening silence. Shane had attached the ring to the very end of the ten-foot-long red ribbon. "I love you, Taylor. Will you marry me?"

Her eyes misted. "I was wondering if you'd ever get around to asking."

He brushed away her tears with his thumb. "I needed to know you could be happy here. With me, doing this."

"I am. I love you, Shane. I'd be happy even without this," she insisted, waving her arm in a wide arc. "This place is like a fantasy for me. One I would never have dreamed if it wasn't for you."

"Are you sure?"

"I am."

"Then put the ring on and give me a second," he said, rushing back inside for a second bag. "Now try this on for size."

Taylor opened the bag and found an identical nameplate to the one he'd just installed.

"You don't have to do it," he insisted when she didn't say anything. "I just thought, that, well…"

"Dr. Taylor Landry," she said, "has a very nice ring to it."

He held her to him. "Goes nicely with the clinic, too. Don't you think?"

Taylor felt her smile all the way down to her toes. Wrapping her arms about his waist, she grinned up at him. "I think another Landry is exactly what the Caleb and Priscilla Landry Clinic needs. We all know there aren't enough Landrys in Jasper."

He smiled. "That's something else we should talk about."

Taylor gave him a mock outraged look. "Are you telling me you won't be the last Landry, after all?"

HARLEQUIN®
INTRIGUE®

WE'LL LEAVE YOU BREATHLESS!

If you've been looking for thrilling tales of contemporary passion and sensuous love stories with taut, edge-of-the-seat suspense—then you'll love Harlequin Intrigue!

Every month, you'll meet six new heroes who are guaranteed to make your spine tingle and your pulse pound. With them you'll enter into the exciting world of Harlequin Intrigue— where your life is on the line and so is your heart!

THAT'S INTRIGUE—
ROMANTIC SUSPENSE
AT ITS BEST!

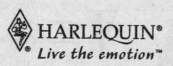

HARLEQUIN®
Live the emotion™

www.eHarlequin.com INTDIR104

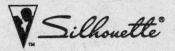

HARLEQUIN®
Presents~

The world's bestselling romance series...
The series that brings you your favorite authors,
month after month:

Helen Bianchin...Emma Darcy
Lynne Graham...Penny Jordan
Miranda Lee...Sandra Marton
Anne Mather...Carole Mortimer
Susan Napier...Michelle Reid

and many more uniquely talented authors!

Wealthy, powerful, gorgeous men...
Women who have feelings just like your own...
The stories you love, set in exotic, glamorous locations...

HARLEQUIN®
Presents~

Seduction and Passion Guaranteed!

HPDIR104

Harlequin Historicals®
Historical Romantic Adventure!

From rugged lawmen and valiant knights to defiant heiresses and spirited frontierswomen, Harlequin Historicals will capture your imagination with their dramatic scope, passion and adventure.

*Harlequin Historicals...
they're too good to miss!*

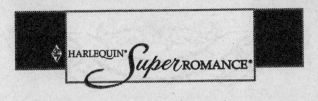
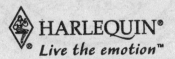